ONE

David Freeman's life was steady, but the inane predictability of his daily schedule was causing his routine to seem *boring*, painfully boring. As he drove west on I-44 from St. Louis toward Springfield, Missouri, he reached for his handheld cassette tape recorder from his briefcase and pushed the record button. "Note to self: my life is boring." He pushed the stop button.

David had always been a nice guy, the one his friends thought of first to set up on a date with their cute cousin. "He's great. You'll just love him," they'd say. "He's a gentleman, a nice guy. And nice guys are hard to find."

He called his mother on a regular basis. He was a good friend with his dad. He worked out regularly. He could cook. He made his bed—even though he lived alone. He got a haircut every two weeks. And he flossed regularly.

David went to college and graduated on time. He paid for his education himself by working part-time and qualifying for a couple of student loans. He'd already paid those loans off, even though he'd been out of college less than five years.

He got along well with his neighbors, his coworkers, and the people at his church, although he didn't have many really close friends, not like he had in high school. Back then, growing up near Fort Wayne, Indiana, the really close friends he had were the other three "hossmen." They weren't the four "horsemen." They were the "*hoss*men." "There's a big difference," David would tell people. "Being a *hossman* was a distinction."

The hossmen played baseball together. They weren't the natural talent guys, the "pretty boys," as they called them. They worked hard for everything they got, and they were notably successful. That's what being a "hoss" was all about. You got down and dirty and worked hard and you succeeded. David wished he could experience a hoss-type alliance with some of his coworkers, but he didn't have that trusting of a relationship with anyone at work yet. He'd been with the company going on four years, but he still felt like he was trying to fit in.

David liked his job with Jay Tools. He was able to travel a lucrative sales route and meet and work with people he found rather interesting. He was paid a regular salary and a commission on what he sold. He could work hard and expect to get paid accordingly. That was one of his most cherished principles of business.

If you work hard, you should get rewarded for it.

Conversely, if you don't work, you shouldn't expect to get paid. His father taught him that. "The laborer is worthy of his hire," Dad would say. Jack Freeman also taught his son many of the other principles that David stood for day after day.

You can't go wrong being an honest man.

Your word is your bond if you shake someone's hand.

If you're going to pay big money for tickets, get a good seat.

David prided himself on being a man of principle. The interested observer might even applaud him for appearing to have all his ducks in a row. "So why do I suddenly consider my life boring?" David said to himself, out loud, while driving. "Maybe it's not really boring." He grabbed the tape recorder and started recording again. "Another note to self: my life is . . . predictable. Day in, day out, the same schedule. The same . . . everything. My life is too predictable. *I'm* too predictable."

He thought maybe it was his name that bothered him. David. Everyone called him David. All the time. *Why can't it be Dave?* he thought. *That was a good baseball name. Dave Stewart. Dave Winfield. Dave Dravecky. Even Davey would have been better than David.* Davey Lopes of the Dodgers was one of his father's favorite players in the '70s. *There weren't many Davids playing ball today. OK, in recent years there have been a couple of really great pitchers: David Cone . . . David Wells. Each of them had even pitched perfect games.* But that still didn't alleviate his feeling that his name was too formal— *too boring. Maybe even the Davids, Cone and Wells, felt the same way about their names,* David thought.

David Norman Freeman. That was his given name. Norman was his grandfather's name on his father's side. He got to know his grandfather surprisingly well, even though he died when David was thirteen.

He frequently reminisced about visiting Grandpa and Grandma's farm just south of Mattoon, Illinois, during the summers. Grandpa Norm wasn't much for long-winded or wordy conversation, but it was evident he had a good grasp of his views on life.

Every once in a while, as if a teachable truth blew with the wind and happened to settle on that Illinois farm, he would share a carefully constructed observation with David. His grandpa never faked superior intelligence by using complicated words. He spoke with simple logic and one-syllable eloquence, making complex issues understandable. David listened when Grandpa Norm spoke.

When most other adults would try to explain life to a younger David, with his sponge-like, wide-eyed imagination, they almost always made things seem too complicated. David would find himself drifting off in boyish fantasy and imagine himself running through the cornfields with no particular purpose except to feel the wind in his face and inhale the aroma of the fresh green cornstalks. Or he might start daydreaming about climbing the combine at his grandparent's farm and pretending it was a fighter jet engaged in air battles over Germany. The crows would become enemy fighters and he'd shoot down every one of them with a make-believe machine gun. However, he didn't wander off when Grandpa Norm spoke to him. When he spoke, David listened with every fiber of his being.

As he got older and the occasion would present itself where he would recall those special conversations with his grandfather, David was drawn not only to the words that he spoke but also his logical convictions as well. That was what impressed David most about the man.

When he got word in October of his eighth grade school year that Grandpa Norm had died, David immediately had tears in his eyes. The family, who only lived six hours away in Indiana, never spent as much time together on the farm in Illinois after Grandpa died, and David missed those days, in the same way that one misses that peaceful, surreal sensation of a dream after getting slapped with the reality of waking up.

David grabbed the tape recorder again and began another diatribe. "Further note to self: my life is not boring or predictable. It's just not that exciting! Not lately, anyway." He tossed the recorder into his briefcase, but then quickly reached over to straighten things up.

This is not to say that David was upset with the way his life was turning out these days. He was very satisfied. He bought a house last fall in South County fairly near the interstate. It was a good investment, and it was a short commute from his house to the Jay Tools corporate office in downtown St. Louis. Or, he could get on I-270 and go south on I-55 toward Memphis or west on I-44 through Springfield and Joplin toward Oklahoma to cover his sales routes. He was heading out on a weeklong business trip today, scheduled to stay in Springfield tonight and meet with a couple of store owners there tomorrow morning, and then head to Joplin for the afternoon. He planned to stay the night in Tulsa on Tuesday so he could make his morning appointments there on Wednesday before heading to Oklahoma City for the afternoon.

David glanced at his day-timer, neatly placed next to his recorder in his open briefcase on the passenger side of his company car. The pens were organized in a plastic protector tucked in the proper section. A Jay Tools notepad was in the adjacent section. The John Grisham novel he was reading was on the right and a couple of his favorite CDs on the left. Everything was in its appropriate place, of course. He skimmed over this week's schedule. *Maybe I'll catch a ball game in Oklahoma City on Wednesday night*, he thought.

David had always loved baseball. He played in high school and at his small college. What he lacked in raw talent he made up for in enthusiasm and hard work. It was the "hoss" way to play ball. He made second team all-conference his junior and senior years in college, but the pros didn't show any interest in his average talents, so he traded in his baseball cleats for salesman's shoes and jumped into his work after graduation.

He applied the "hoss" ethic he learned from playing ball to his sales job and moved up the corporate ladder fairly quickly. Last year, David was honored to be named Jay Tools top regional salesman. He was awarded a company car, a tan late model Chevrolet Caprice with a license plate that read JTOOLS 1.

He stayed active in sports after college, but he was reduced to playing softball for the company team and also for the church team. Softball just couldn't compare to baseball in David's mind. It was fun, a chance to get some exercise, but playing baseball was an experience like no other to David.

Baseball is the game of life, David mused. He spent a great deal of time philosophizing about this theory while driving along the Missouri and Oklahoma interstates. The steady rhythmic road hum can put a man's mind on cruise control without something to occupy his thoughts.

Baseball is an opportunity to succeed against great odds. When a player is batting, he's competing against nine people all working to see him fail. But half the game, a player is one of those nine people trying to foil that one person at bat.

Also, in baseball, David knew, the player needs to develop a sense of where to stand, how to stand, where to move, and what to do when the action comes to you. It's preparation. It's teamwork. It's skill. It's luck. It's life. It's baseball.

Baseball is also like life in that it's a game of principles. There's a *right* way to play the game, David often told himself, and anyone who would listen. You can play it wrong, but you probably won't be successful at it. And if you play the game the way it's supposed to be played, you can experience an incredible depth to the game. Few people are willing to sink their hearts into the game with that much insight.

David continued to think as he drove. As an example, there

were several guys on David's church softball team who hadn't played much ball. They weren't able to scoop up the ground balls very consistently, and if they did manage to field a grounder cleanly, they didn't always know where to throw the ball. Each time a player made an error like that, it was like giving the opposing team an extra out for that inning, bringing up a prime principle a successful ballplayer always adheres to:

*Know what you're going to do with the ball before
it's hit to you, field it cleanly, and make the play.*

A good player just won't give the other team more than three outs per inning. That was part of the right way to play. The winning way. The baseball way. What fired David up the most was when the inexperienced players on his team made mistakes, but didn't learn from their mistakes and make the right play the next time. Making the same mistakes over and over again showed you didn't care, and caring about the game, whether you were a skilled player or not, was one of David's most sacred principles.

It might have been a trivial formality, but one game, one of the "rookies," as David called them, was wearing his baseball cap backward. "I admit that I'm from the old school when it comes to baseball customs," David would say. "Wearing a baseball cap backward is a sacrilege to baseball tradition." That day, he barked at the player: "Hey, Slim! This is a ball club, not a rap group." The greenhorn looked surprised, but he knew what David was referring to and turned his hat around to the baseball way. Next game, the kid had his hat on backward again. David didn't say anything this time, but he surmised that the guy just didn't care.

David always went out of his way to care. Not only about baseball, but also about what he considered the many important fundamental areas of a successful person's personal life.

David always held tightly to his beliefs, his principles. Of course his grandfather influenced him in that regard, but so did his dad. By today's standards, people might describe both of them as rigid or stiff, but David always looked at them as solid. Their principles were so rooted and genuine that they could listen to another person's opinion and size it up rather quickly as to whether they believed the same way or whether they took a different slant. Sure, they changed their minds on rare occasions, but the evidence that there was a *better* way certainly would have to be monumental before that occurred.

David had been developing his principles over the years, and been forced by evidentiary logic to adjust some of them—like women working outside the home. Sylvia, David's mom, didn't work outside the home while he was growing up. His grandmother never did have a job outside the home. They both worked hard doing the cooking and the cleaning and the "women things," as folks used to call them before the politically correct police convinced everyone they were always listening over people's shoulders.

However, David had a talk with his mom one quiet evening a couple of years ago and she voiced some regrets that she was never afforded the opportunity to go to college and pursue a professional vocation.

She worked a couple of years as a switchboard operator after high school and married David's dad after he got out of the Air Force. She held down the switchboard job another couple of years until David was born, but she stayed home to raise him from then on. College then became an impossible, impractical dream in her distant memory, and she had harbored those blurred career dreams for many years, but not to the point that she was angry or resentful. She merely wondered what it might have been like to explore a professional field like medicine or law or even business.

A layer of blindness was chipped away from his mind that

day by his mother's sincerity, and he rearranged his principle that "a woman's place is in the home." If and when he ever did get married, he figured he'd insist that his wife pursue her dreams too. If they had children along the way, they'd tackle that situation when they came to it.

Marriage seemed a long way off to David, although he was open to the idea. He dated some in high school and college and had a couple of steady girlfriends. He thought he was serious about one girl in college, but she drifted off to Indiana University with a law student.

He always wondered what falling in love with the "right girl" would feel like. He asked his dad one time when he was about fourteen and all his dad, Jack, could say was, "You'll know." That seemed like a dumb answer, but Jack explained that that was what Grandpa Norm had told him and that it was the truth. He said David was going to have to experience it for himself. True love seemed like a distant lighthouse on a faraway shore at this juncture in his life.

David sighed and picked up the recorder one more time. "Last note: my life *is* predictable, not very exciting, and maybe a little boring. I'm set in my ways of thinking, but it's not that bad. I've got good principles. I'm a nice guy. And I'm still a hoss! And I've got customers in Springfield to think about. And I'm hungry. It's almost supper time."

He pushed the stop button with authority, put the recorder back in the briefcase, and closed the lid with a slam. He pulled off the interstate at the Waynesville exit and headed for the Burger Royal.

David parked his car neatly between two other cars, perfectly inside the white lines. He brushed a thin streak of dust off the dashboard and adjusted the mirror so he could see to fix his tie. He looked into his own eyes, and they told him the truth: he could always see the bottom-line truth in his own eyes. *I am principled and predictable and set in my ways,* he thought. *And regular people usually call that boring.*

* * * * *

Joani Givens was being dragged along today, like some kind of ornament, on a drug run by her manipulative roommate, whom everyone called Snake. She was reluctant company, but the best Snake could muster, especially since it was Joani's car they were driving. He ran his stuff out of St. Louis, primarily marijuana and cocaine. Snake's customer network was mostly small-time scum who distributed to high school and junior high kids in the St. Louis area and in unpretentious towns along I-44. He was a lowlife, and Joani had nothing better going for her today, so she agreed to hang out with Snake, mostly so she could keep an eye on her car.

Today, they were in Lebanon, Missouri. Snake was checking up on some rat that had stiffed him. He had used a couple of local thugs to help convince the rodent that he had better pay his debts. They needed to get some gas for the drive back to St. Louis. Snake also needed to make a couple of additional phone calls.

They pulled into the Gas Stop. After he fueled the black Camaro, Snake pulled the car up to the store so he could make his calls on his cell phone.

"Just sit there and shut up!" he growled sternly at Joani. "I gotta make a couple of calls. I've put up with too much crap already today. I don't need any from you."

TWO

David decided to go inside rather than go through the drive-through. He stretched his arms and legs as he got out of the car. It had already been a long day. He had met with customers in the St. Louis area during regular business hours. A lot of walking, talking and driving.

I want to have a burger tonight. I've had a lot of chicken lately, and the change might taste good.

David went inside and hit the bathroom to wash his hands before going to the counter to order his food. A teenage boy, obviously in a hurry, was at the sink washing his hands. He slapped the button on the hands-free air dryer and energetically rubbed his hands together to try to dry them. Impatient at how long the process was taking, he ended up wiping his hands on his jeans and then rushed out of the bathroom. *At least he washed his hands*, David thought. *I've seen so many*

people who don't wash their hands after using a public restroom.
As he went to dry his hands, he read the instructions printed
on the dryer.

Shake excess water off hands.

Push button.

Rub hands vigorously under dryer until dry.

Someone had scratched on the machine:

Wipe hands on pants.

At least the boy was following directions. David's hands
were completely dry with just a few extra seconds under the
dryer.

There was a middle-aged couple in line in front of him at
the counter. They were having trouble deciding what they
wanted. *Like you don't already know what's on the menu at
these places,* David thought. David waited patiently until they
figured out their best deal. The couple finally made their de-
cision, moved down the line, and a teenage boy with freckles
took David's order. The boy seemed like he'd worked there for
a while. He was very efficient and professional. "May I help
you?" he asked.

"I'll have the Double Whammer combo with just lettuce,
tomato, and mayonnaise."

"Just lettuce, tomato, and mayonnaise?" the boy queried.

"Yes," David answered in his usual polite way.

The boy called in the order over the microphone, handed
David a receipt, and took off toward the back. David looked
at the receipt and noticed the boy had charged him too much.
The subtotal was $4.23 and the sign read "Double Whammer
Combo $3.99." He must have looked confused while inspect-

ing the receipt because an older lady also working behind the counter asked if he needed anything.

"I think he charged me too much," David said.

He handed the receipt to the lady, who inspected it and said, "That's a Double Whammer with cheese combo. Four twenty-three."

"That's not what I ordered," he replied.

"What did you order?"

"I wanted the Double Whammer combo with just lettuce, tomato, and mayonnaise. No cheese."

Making the correction on David's order, the woman repeated his words into the microphone. She handed him twenty cents, said she was sorry for the inconvenience, and looked to take the next customer's order. David hesitated and then turned back to the lady. "I'm sorry," he said. "I know it's a little thing, but you didn't give me enough change back."

"You gotta figure in the tax," the woman replied briskly, as if to explain away the entire situation in one statement.

"No, the combo with cheese is $4.23 and the Double Whammer *without* cheese combo is $3.99. Four twenty-three minus three ninety-nine is twenty-four cents. I know it's just a little thing, but I am right, aren't I?"

"Like I said," the woman bristled, "you have to figure in the tax."

"The tax has nothing to do with it," he said with a slightly louder and confident voice.

"OK," she sighed as she opened the cash register.

"OK, here's your four cents, sir." The lady turned to wait on the next customer and spoke out loud to a couple of teenage employees as well as to two customers in line behind David. "What a day," she gasped. "That's the second one of those I've had today."

David turned back toward her. "Were you referring to me? Am I *one of those*? You mean a *customer* don't you?" The woman started to speak, but he interrupted her. "You do believe that in business the customer is always right, don't you?"

The woman smiled a timid smile and said, "Yes, sir, I do."

"Especially when the customer is right. I can't believe I'd get such a hassle over something so little." He suddenly realized he was making a scene. The rest of the customers seated in the restaurant had looked up because they had overheard everything he had said.

David filled up his cup of coke at the drink self-service station and took his Double Whammer combo bag and left the Burger Royal without looking at anyone. Someone from behind the counter offered a "Thank you!" but he refused to acknowledge them.

He got to his car and embarrassment snuck up on him for making such a fuss. He tried to justify his actions by thinking out loud: "But I was right, and the woman was wrong." He didn't care as much about the four cents as he cared about being told he was wrong when he knew he was right. It was as if the woman was insistent about showing him that she knew more about the fast-food industry than David did. However, the principle here was that the situation wasn't a fast-food problem, it was a math problem. And then it turned into a customer relations problem.

David had always set high standards for himself when dealing with his own customers. Sure, he made mistakes from time to time. He was only human. But when he found out he was wrong, he made sure the situation was corrected. It was better to lose a little on a deal and still have the customer's respect than to overlook a mistake and pay for it by losing a customer.

One time in particular, David had overcharged a store owner for an item that was on special that month. The customer didn't bring it up, but David noticed it when he went over his paperwork at the end of the week. He returned to the store the next week and pointed out the discrepancy. The store owner was rather shocked and pleased that he wanted to give him a refund. That customer had become one of David's biggest clients to this day, largely because he displayed some integrity early on in the relationship.

David recognized the true value of his customers to his livelihood. The woman at the Burger Royal displayed what he called the "talk show mentality" when dealing with him.

The talk show mentality was something David came up with after watching a couple of those daytime TV talk shows on his day off. *I couldn't believe the problems that those guests had, the subjects they were covering, and the anger that most people were displaying,* he thought. The one common denominator each of the guests and each of the people in the audience had was this: Right or wrong, my opinion is still right!

Some of their opinions were based on incredibly selfish motives or double standards. Husbands wanted their wives to be understanding if they went out and partied all night while the wife stayed home. Homely looking husbands were upset that their wives had gained a lot of weight since they had gotten married and objected that their wives weren't looking up to their standards. Adult daughters complained that their lives were messed up because their mothers were strict with them when they were growing up. It seemed to David that everyone was blaming everyone else for their situations, and no one was willing to take a look at their own life first and consider any changes *they* should make. And then when evidence was presented that they were totally in the wrong, they would take the fallback position of claiming the other person was lying.

When one audience guest stood up and said the on-stage guest should "get a life," David heeded the advice himself and turned off the TV and retreated inside his headphones with a Vince Gill album. He reasoned *Life is so much more manage-*

able when you have well-thought-out principles that you choose to live by.

As he drove away from the Burger Royal and feasted on the less-than-perfect burger and the now chilly fries, he found himself less and less upset with the situation with each passing mile. Then he realized he'd originally paid $4.52 for the Double Whammer combo with tax. The new price of the "without cheese" combo was $4.27. The lady actually owed him twenty-*five* cents. He had forgotten to figure in the tax on the twenty-four cents difference, even though the lady had mentioned taxes. David laughed out loud. "Maybe I should go back and lodge another complaint," he said. David laughed out loud again. The situation was pretty amusing after all. And in the end, he reasoned, he may be boring and predictable, but he still had a good sense of humor.

David hoped the lady learned something from the situation and didn't feel that he was the kind to hold a grudge. There were principles to this dilemma though, and he felt satisfied about standing his ground. He just hoped it didn't ruin the lady's day. He didn't think it would be wise to go back to that Burger Royal again. Thankfully, there were many other restaurants along I-44. He traveled this road so many times he thought he knew them all.

The whole Burger Royal situation had taken over his mind so much that he had forgotten to get gas at the Waynesville exit. As he sipped the last few drops of his cola, he glanced at the gas gauge. Both the cup and the gas tank were very near empty. The Lebanon exit was only a couple of miles up the road. *I'll get gas there,* he thought. *Thank God I noticed that. I need a smooth ride from here to Springfield.*

THREE

David exited the interstate and headed for the Gas Stop station. He might have gotten gas there before, but he wasn't sure. The place was fairly busy, but he was able to pull to a pump right away. He began filling his Caprice with regular fuel. He thought one more time about the Burger Royal incident and again laughed quietly to himself.

Cars were pulling in and out of the Gas Stop. Since customers were starting to form backup lines at the pumps, and David was paying with cash, he decided to fill his tank and then pull up to the building to pay so the next customer wouldn't have to wait. After filling up, he pulled up to the building and into the only available space, one next to a black Camaro.

The Camaro had some bumps in the body and looked like it had been repainted a flat black to cover its original color, but it still appeared to be a really fast and rugged car.

As David got out of his Caprice to pay for the gas, he couldn't help but notice the young lady in her twenties in the passenger seat of the black Camaro next to him. They both did a quick double take at each other. At first glance, he was struck by her natural, rugged beauty. She had long straight auburn hair and piercing green eyes. He half smiled at her and nodded, but didn't want her to feel like he was staring.

As he pulled the convenience store door open, a tall, thin angry man barged his way out. He swept past David and didn't say "excuse me" or even look at him as he blasted through the door on his way to the Camaro. He was obviously a tough character, dressed in a plain black T-shirt, black jeans, and black biker boots. His long, dirty blond hair and beard were unkempt and shaggy. David let him pass and went inside to pay. As the door shut behind him, he heard the man curse and tell the girl in the Camaro something about his cell phone dying and needing to go back into the store and use the store's old pay phone.

David reached the counter and told the attendant he had the gas on pump number six. "That'll be nineteen-fifty," the clerk said. David gave the man a twenty and waited patiently. As the worker was giving David his fifty cents change and the receipt, the tall, thin angry man burst through the door and headed to the back of the store. David and the attendant both flinched when he smacked open the door. *Quite an entrance,* David thought, but then moved on and calmly stuffed his change and the receipt in his shirt pocket. *No hassles this time—not like at the Burger Royal. That's the way it should be.*

As he turned toward the door, he could hear the angry man's agitated voice as he argued with someone on the phone at the back of the store. David didn't pay much attention to his words, except to note that he was angry with someone. From their brief encounter, he surmised that the man's anger might be a constant emotion dominating his rough demeanor.

Outside, David walked around the front of his car and grabbed the door handle. He caught another quick innocent glance at the auburn-haired lady in the Camaro. However, she startled him when she spoke to him in an excited, breathy voice. "Which way you headed on the interstate?"

"West," he said with a stutter as he opened his car door.

"You gotta help me!" She started crawling quickly over the Camaro's console into the driver's seat. "There's a rest stop a couple of miles up the road. Please meet me there. I need your help. Please!" The agile young beauty started the car and hammered it into reverse. She looked at David one more time and pleaded, "The rest stop. Please. You gotta help me. It could be life or death!"

She gave it some gas and backed out of the parking space, squealing the tires. She shoved it into first gear and squealed the tires again as she headed for the Gas Stop exit, the road, and the interstate.

David climbed into his car, bewildered. "What a day! People are *crazy*," he muttered to himself. He started his car and backed up considerably slower than the Camaro. As he shifted into drive, out of the corner of his eye, he caught a glimpse of the tall angry man in black as he rushed out the door and into the parking lot. The man cursed and threw a pack of cigarettes to the ground. David avoided any eye contact with him as he calmly drove toward the same exit the Camaro had taken.

In his rearview mirror he noticed the man in black watching as the Camaro with the auburn-haired driver sped away. Because of the rolling-hilled contour of the land, it was impossible to tell if the Camaro went east on the interstate toward St. Louis or west toward Springfield. But the man in black was clearly livid that the girl would take off and leave him at the gas station. David wanted no part of this guy.

* * * * *

Snake reached down to pick up his pack of cigarettes. He cursed again. He was incensed. "That . . . God, she's gonna get it!" He turned to go back inside to call one of his local henchmen and demand that they drop what they were doing and take him back to St. Louis. As he did, he noticed a late model tan Caprice leaving the Gas Stop slowly. The license plate read JTOOLS 1.

That was easy to remember.

FOUR

David headed west on the interstate. *What a scene!* His normal, calm, and even boring life had suddenly taken a turn toward exciting and mysterious. *Is that girl serious? Does she really expect me to meet her at the rest stop? What would I say to her? What does she have in mind? I'm not sure if I should get involved. Maybe I should call the police.* David saw a road sign that read "Rest Area One Mile." *There is a rest stop a couple of miles down the road, just like the girl said.* He had probably passed it a dozen times before, but never noticed it.

David had to make up his mind immediately if he was going to meet her at the rest stop because the exit was coming up fast. He quickly reasoned that he wasn't the kind of person to desert someone in a time of need, and this girl was obviously in need. "This is crazy," he said as he flipped on his turn signal and slowed down as he approached the rest stop exit.

He didn't see the Camaro at first. *Is she really going to be here?* Then he spotted it toward the back of the rest area, in the shade, away from the buildings. He approached with some caution, not knowing if the girl was actually in trouble or if she was luring him into a trap of some sort.

He parked two spaces away from the black car. The girl got out and approached his passenger-side window. He rolled down the electric window, but only halfway. She leaned over and rested her bare forearms on the window. "You don't know how glad I am that you met me here," she began.

"What's this all about?" David asked.

"I've been trying to get away from that jerk for a long time. He's into all kinds of scary stuff. He's turned into the meanest guy I've ever met."

"What do you want with me?"

"Look, my aunt and uncle live near Springfield. Could I hitch a ride with you to their place? I know this all sounds pretty strange, but I can explain it on the way. Please. You're my only help."

David hesitated, but only for a second. "OK. You don't want to leave your car here, do you?"

"I can't just leave it here," she said, assessing her options, "but there's a place up the road I can ditch it for a while. I can't take it to the farm. Not right away. I gotta hide it for a while. Follow me up the road a ways and I'll take care of it. I really appreciate your help. You'll never know . . . "

David nodded in rushed agreement. "OK, let's get going. Something tells me your friend isn't too happy about you taking off with his car."

The girl got back in the Camaro and revved it. She backed out and took off toward the rest area exit. David glanced around to see if anyone at the rest area had been watching their conversation. Fortunately, he didn't see anyone. A couple of trucks were parked on the other side of the large lot. There were two cars parked a little closer, but drivers were nowhere around. He followed the Camaro out of the rest stop and onto the highway.

They drove the speed limit. David was glad of that. The girl looked like she was in a hurry, but at least she had the good sense to not draw attention to herself. The tall, angry man may have called the police and reported his car stolen. That thought raised David's apprehension level. He was in over his head for sure, but something told him that he was doing the right thing.

David tried to dig deeper and reason why he was getting involved in this bizarre situation. Was it because the girl was pretty? No, she wasn't really his type. She looked like she'd been around the block, to say the least, and seen a rougher side of life, one David had never been around.

Was he trying to be some sort of knight in shining armor who rescues the damsel in distress, David asked himself. That scenario didn't make much sense. He wasn't that dramatic.

David finally told himself that he was getting involved because someone needed his help. That was, after all, another one of his tightly held tenets.

When someone needs your help,
help in the best way you can.

David went out of his way to offer quality help to people whenever he could. A local inner-city youth center had advertised that they needed an English tutor for junior high kids. The tutoring session was on Mondays, and he knew if he committed to teaching the kids, he'd have to give up his Monday bowling night in the winter and also playing for the company softball team during the spring. It wasn't that hard to choose which road to travel. He wasn't that much of a bowler. He only did it because it was something to do and it got him out with people. And he didn't mind giving up the softball for one season. He'd played ball every summer since he was eight years old. He figured a season off might do him some good. He might appreciate the game even more when he came back the next spring.

Secretly, though, he looked forward to helping those kids learn to read better. He had done the same thing while he was in high school through a Big Brother/Big Sister program in his hometown. David was thrilled when his group of eight boys were tested at program's end and it was discovered that every one of them showed reading improvement of at least two full grade levels. The head of the program was so impressed that he told David if he decided to become a full-time teacher someday, he'd give him a good reference. David kept that in mind, but never pursued a teaching degree in college. He felt his best talents were in sales. And he was satisfied that he'd pursued that career. Still, he felt gratified that he had helped a few youngsters improve their lot in life. He knew that good reading skills were essential to someone making his or her life a success in this world. "Leaders are readers," his dad would say. He would back that up by always having a new book to read. David wasn't as avid a reader as his dad, just yet, because other interests took higher priority in his life, but he knew the importance of pouring himself into all types of literature.

Helping people learn to read was certainly a noble cause, but the bottom-line principle of today's situation was this:

Helping people less fortunate than you or people in trouble is—or should be—a requirement of all people.

There may be a time in your own life when you'll need a helping hand. What goes around, comes around. These were all part of the ideology of a person of principle—and that was David Freeman.

Still, here he was driving down the road, following a lady he didn't know, in a Camaro that technically was stolen, to an unknown destination. It seemed daringly frightening, and yet important. It certainly wasn't boring.

FIVE

The Camaro drove past the first exit. It dawned on David that he didn't even know which exit the girl was going to take. Come to think of it, he didn't even know her name. *Did she say her relatives lived near Springfield? Would she be going there to drop the car off, or maybe another place?* David's life was a little more predictable than this. He was still wondering if he had done the right thing in trying to help this girl. Just then, the Camaro's turn signal came on. The next exit was a mile up the road.

David followed the Camaro through the exit. They came to a stop and turned right. The road looked like it might lead to a nearby town, but David wasn't sure. He had traveled this highway many times, but had never gotten off at this exit because there weren't any modern facilities for food services or a working gas station. There was an abandoned gas station at the exit, and David almost ran into the back of the Camaro as the girl turned abruptly into it. She pulled the car around to the back of the building. He waited for her in the parking lot, his engine on idle but his mind itching to get going down the road. Grass was growing in the cracks in the pavement as a testament to how long the station had been closed. There was a Coke machine out front, but it had long been empty of refreshment.

The auburn-haired girl strolled around from the back of the building carrying her purse in one hand and a medium-sized duffel bag over the same shoulder. David closed his briefcase and set it on the backseat. She trotted up to the car, her long hair bouncing in the breeze. He unlocked the passenger side door. She opened the door and tossed her duffel on top of his briefcase in the back seat. She dropped down in the front seat with her purse and told David the guy who used to own this station was an old friend of the family. "He's been out of business for a year or so," she explained. "He'll know whose car it is. He worked on it a couple of summers ago. Besides, there's not much traffic on this exit. The car'll be safe here."

David turned and faced the girl. "I've got a lot of questions to ask you."

"Do you think we could get back on the road? The further I get from that car right now, the better. I'll tell you everything. I'm just glad to get away from Snake."

"*Snake?*" David repeated.

"Let's get going. I'll tell you all about it."

David shifted into drive and pulled out of the deserted gas station parking lot, kicking up tiny stones. He got on the freeway entrance ramp and started gaining speed. They had not seen even one car since they got off the highway and the girl hid the Camaro.

"I guess the first question is, What's your name?" David asked.

"I'm Joani Givens."

"And Snake?"

"He's the guy I've been livin' with the past couple of years. I've been wantin' to get away from him for a while now. I never had the chance until today. I kinda had it all planned out in my head, but you were the missing piece. You looked like you might help if you thought I was in some kind of trouble." Joani went to light up a cigarette. "Mind if I smoke?"

He hesitated. "I really don't . . . " David wasn't entirely sure how to object. "I mean, I'm sort of allergic to smoke."

"I've been meanin' to quit anyway. This is as good a time as any to stop." She stuffed the cigarette pack into her purse and leaned against the corner of the door and the back of the seat, letting out a hefty sigh. "I don't know. I just feel like my life is going to take a turn for the better now."

"By the way," David continued, "where are we going?"

"I'd like to go to my aunt and uncle's house on this side of Springfield. I don't know where you're going, but I'm glad you were headin' west. I know this sounds crazy . . . "

"Crazy, yeah," he muttered.

" . . . but if you just take me to my aunt and uncle's, I won't ask any more favors of you."

David nodded and let the silence take over for an uncomfortable minute or two while he collected his thoughts. "So your name is Joani and you've been living with Snake and now you're running away from him. Is that right?"

"It's more like escaping," Joani reasoned. "He wasn't so bad when I first met him, but lately he's gotten really out of control. He's a drug dealer and I think he's been a petty thief for a while, but he must be using his own stuff lately, and that's made him crazy."

Crazy, David thought. *There's that word again.* "Uh, where'd you meet him?" David asked.

"I was workin' as a waitress in this junky bar in St. Louis.

He would come in to shoot pool with the guys. He was a loud-mouth, and he drank too much. But he wasn't any worse than any of the other guys I'd been around. We got to talkin'. One thing led to another. I needed a place to stay. He told me I could share some space at his apartment down the street from the bar. I said OK. That's about it. Hey, I never got your name."

"Oh, it's David Freeman." He didn't feel like obliging her with any details of *his* mundane life, as if she could relate to it or even believe how ordinary his life was. Still, she posed several questions to him anyway.

"You from St. Louis?"

"Yes. I'm a salesman for a tool company. I travel this road a lot. Also down to Memphis."

"You married?"

"No. I'm ... "

Joani interrupted. "You're waitin' for the right girl, the perfect house and happily ever after, aren't you?"

"Well, yeah." David had envisioned those things for his life, but hearing it explained that way by Joani made it sound dreadfully conventional, and boring.

"Well, good luck, David. More power to ya. Ya got my vote for agreein' to meet me at the rest area. Boy, you don't know how lucky I am that you pulled right next to us. And then Snake had to go back inside. And then you came out." She moved her hands in front of her from one side to the other to describe the sequence of events. "And then I just did it." She clapped her hands in triumph. "I asked you to meet me at the rest stop and then drove away." Again, she motioned forward with her hand. "Yep, I just drove away and left that clod there. Man, he must be ticked."

"You think he might miss his car?" David asked.

"It's not *his* car. It's *my* car. His got wrecked last week. It's gettin' fixed. Mine doesn't look that nice from the outside, but it'll motor."

"Why'd you leave it back there at that abandoned gas station if it's *your* car? Won't you want it at your aunt's house?"

"Nah, not for a while. I gotta hide for a while 'til I find a way to get some money together so I can head to L.A. or Seattle or Montana, some place far away from St. Louis. I'll wait 'til the heat's off and go back and pick it up. It'll be safe there. No one goes around there anymore. One of my aunt's old neighbors owns the property. Even if he goes out there, he'll know the car is mine. He worked on it enough." Joani slumped down and rested her head on the back of the seat.

David still had a morbid talk show-like curiosity about this girl's life. "So this guy Snake won't come looking for you?"

"God, I hope not." She sat bolt upright. "Nah, he won't bother. He can always find another girl to push around." She slumped down in the seat again. "I do know a little about his operation, but I don't know *that* much. He's not gonna worry about me. He'll probably think I flipped out and that I'm not worth goin' after. Yeah, that's it." She was trying hard to convince herself that was the way it was.

David had kept his eyes pretty much on the road, although he did glance at Joani periodically. She had an appealing, although rough, face. She jumped around a lot in her seat as if the adrenaline was flowing because of her daringly successful escape. She was like a puppy that had been on a chain for a long time and was just released to run through the park.

He had more questions, but not necessarily about the situation with Snake. He thought he pretty much understood all of that from her short explanation. Instead, he was curious about Joani's life. What she thought about. What she believed in. *How was she raised? Do her parents know what kind of life she is living?* He wondered if he would have time to find out or if he was only going to serve as courier dispatch and drop her off at her aunt's home and that would be the end of it.

The sign said: Springfield 12 Miles. "I'm not sure what exit it is," Joani said. "The town is called Fair Grove. If you could take me to my aunt's farm there, I promise I won't ask any more favors."

David looked over at her. "This has been an interesting day. Honestly, this kind of situation has never happened to me before."

"Maybe that's good, Dave. You don't seem the type to . . . " She hesitated. "Oh, never mind."

"What do you mean?" he pressed. "I'm not the type to what?"

"You don't seem to be the type to lead a tough life. You look like you'd help somebody along the way, but you've probably never been in any real trouble before."

"Oh, I've been in trouble before."

"I'll bet you've never spent one night in jail," she said.

"Well, no," David admitted. "But I've . . ." He wanted to boast about the extremes in his life, but he knew there weren't any. He glanced again at Joani. She was looking at David with her eyebrows raised. He looked back ahead to the road and then glanced at her again. She was still looking at him with the same expression.

"You've what?" she asked.

David knew that his life had been pretty tame compared to the few minutes of Joani's personal history she had just told him. "All right," he admitted. "I do lead a pretty dull life, and I've never really been in trouble. You win."

Joani gave out an air-punch toward David's shoulder. "That's OK, Dave. I think you just might be the winner here."

They passed an exit sign that read: Exit 88 Route 125 Fair Grove One Mile.

"That's my exit comin' up," she said.

* * * * *

Snake's flunky drove up to the Gas Stop in a beat-up Ford Fairlane, two tone in color: blue and rust. "This piece of junk the only thing you could find?" Snake said, disgustedly.

"It's my sister's car, Snake. It's the only thing I could get on such short notice."

"Will it make it to St. Louis?" he muttered.

"Oh yeah. It'll make it to St. Louis just fine, Snake."

"All right. Then let's move. I got business in St. Louis."

SIX

David followed along as Joani gave directions off the Fair Grove exit.

"I guess I haven't forgotten the way to my aunt's house," she said. "I used to spend summers here when I was a kid." Joani's excitement seemed to be building as she anticipated her homecoming. There was a soft smile on her face now and a calm tone in her voice. Her aura of roughness was smoothing out.

"I used to spend a lot of time at my grandpa's farm in Illinois when I was growing up," David said. "My folks and I used to spend at least a couple of weeks there every year."

"I'd spend the whole summer here when I was a kid," Joani said. "My mom would drop me off when school was out and wouldn't pick me up 'til Labor Day."

"Didn't she visit you during the summer?"

"Well, sure, but only for a couple of days at a time. Then,

she'd head back to the city to make a living."

"What kind of work did your mom do?" David asked.

"She was a working girl," Joani replied, hesitantly, as if David was so naive he wouldn't know what that meant. "You know, a lady of the evening."

"I knew what you meant." From the tone of his voice, she could sense his concern for her having grown up in that kind of environment.

"Don't get upset, Dave. It may not have been the best of jobs, but it was a living. She kept telling me that she never ever wanted me to get into that line of work. She harped on me to get a good education and find something respectable to do so I could make a decent life for myself. She felt like she didn't have any other way to turn because her folks had died when she was young and she got tossed around between foster homes 'til she ran away from the last one when she was sixteen." Joani shook her head. "Sixteen years old and on her own in the big city. Not much else but prostitution for her to do."

"Where's your mom today?" he asked.

"She's dead," Joani said as abruptly as her death had probably happened. "She got sick right before I spent my last summer on the farm, the summer after I graduated from high school. She died one night in our apartment. All alone. I was here on the farm enjoyin' the fresh air and wide open spaces, and she just curled up and died one hot night in St. Louis in that run-down apartment of ours."

Joani wiped her nose with the back of her hand.

"Joani, you don't have to tell me all this. I didn't mean to bring up bad memories."

"No. It's OK. It's the farm. The farm brings back the memories of my mom. I really don't think of her that often, except her reminders of never wanting me to follow in her footsteps." Joani curled her lips. "Huh. Working as a waitress in a crummy bar and livin' with a dope dealer. Not too much higher on the social ladder than call girl, is it?" She quickly turned her attention to giving directions. "Turn right up here. It's about a mile down the road."

The road was smooth for a farm road. Not much rain in this part of Missouri this spring. The roads were level and drier than normal. The winter potholes had been graded down by tractors and pickups. What little gravel there was crunched under the tires and kicked up a little dust. David figured his car would have to be washed tomorrow before he headed to Joplin.

Joani's face brightened noticeably when she saw the farmhouse. "There it is. There it is," she gushed. "Up there on the right. I haven't been here for three, four years, but it hasn't changed a bit. There it is." She was like a kindergartner spying the yellow school bus down the road coming to pick her up on the first day of school. She didn't know what to expect, but she was excited about the possibilities.

David drove down the narrow dirt and grass path to the circle drive in front of the house and one-car garage. Three large oak trees shaded the small yard surrounding the modest white farm home. The front porch sported three rocking chairs that reminded David of the times he sat on the porch at Grandpa Norm's home with him and his dad and watched the sun set behind the cornfield. A large old red barn rose high in the air a hundred yards south of the house. A fenced-in area near the barn confined a couple dozen pigs.

As they pulled to the top of the circle drive, Joani jumped out of the car before David could even break to a complete stop. "Aunt June!" she yelled. "Aunt June!"

The front door opened as they pulled into the circle. A large, kindly slightly gray-haired woman in her fifties opened the squeaky screen door as Joani called out to her. "Joani? My land, Joani!"

Joani ran through the open front gate and down the twenty

yards to the front porch of the old house. She leaped up three steps and clomped past the first rocking chair, her arms wide open to give Aunt June a homecoming hug. June returned the hug with equal enthusiasm, first wiping her hands on her apron, then hugging, then wiping her eyes with the apron, then hugging again.

David parked the car and picked up Joani's purse and duffel bag that she had left in the car as she ran toward the house. He walked up the well-worn concrete path to the front porch, and the memories of his own days on the farm flooded his mind. Listening to the Cubs games on the huge old radio with Dad and Grandpa Norm. Mr. Nichols, Grandpa's closest neighbor, coming up the walk in his best brown suit and tie to inform the family that his cow had birthed a calf that morning and his wife had birthed a son that afternoon. David's grandma said later that she didn't even know that Mrs. Nichols, a rather stout woman, was even pregnant. Also, the time when one of the Elliott boys had gotten a real coconut and came over to share some of the tender white meat with the family. Grandpa Norm had slowly cut a small piece with his pocket knife and chewed it for several minutes, savoring all of the juice from the exotic fruit. He simply nodded his head and said, "Not bad. Not bad at all," as if he was pleased with the experience, but that it wouldn't be necessary for him to have any more raw coconut for the rest of his life.

David sat the bags on the porch as Joani and Aunt June unhooked their embrace. They had been talking and crying. David caught the last of the conversation. Aunt June remarked, "I'm so glad you're rid of that man. He was no good."

"I know," Joani said. "I know." The two turned toward David. "Aunt June, this is Dave. I forgot your last name."

"David Freeman," he replied.

"He's a knight in shining armor," Joani said with a smile. David felt a twinge of pride at Joani's comment, that she considered him chivalrous.

"Nice to meet you, Mr. Freeman," Aunt June said, wiping her hands again on her apron and reaching to shake his hand. She had a firm grip, like she'd been milking cows and doing farm labor all her life. "Thanks so much for helping Joani. Would you care to come in and share supper with us?"

"I really need to get going. I've got business in Springfield tomorrow morning and then I'm off to Joplin and then Oklahoma for a couple of days."

"Can I fix you a sandwich to take on your way?"

"No. I'm fine. Thank you. I really should be going."

Joani turned to her aunt. "I'm gonna walk Dave to his car."

"OK. Thank you again, Mr. Freeman. Thanks for giving Joani a ride."

"No problem. Nice to meet you. You've got a nice farm. It reminds me of my grandparents' farm in Illinois."

Aunt June gushed. "Oh, sometimes it's a headache. But it's home. Come back and visit anytime."

"Thank you. I just might do that." He turned to walk toward his car. Joani walked beside him along the narrow concrete walkway and brushed her arm against his. It was really the first time they'd touched.

"You really are welcome to come back some time. Anytime. Maybe you can tell me about the wild and crazy life of a salesman."

"My life is really pretty tame," he said. "But I like it that way, I suppose." Joani's entire disposition had changed since she saw the farmhouse in the distance down the dirt road. The fear and anxiety that etched her face was gone, replaced by a peace that only the fresh air and sunshine of God's outdoors could provide. David looked into her eyes, which now seemed soft, instead of piercing, like they were back when he had first glanced at her at the Gas Stop. "You really made my day today." They both laughed, relieved that the intensity of the adventure was apparently behind them. "I thought it was going to be just another day on the road, listening to talk radio and motivational tapes. You gonna be OK?"

She nodded and smiled a placid smile. "I am now. Thanks. Thanks for going out of your way and helping me."

"I just hope everything works out for you."

"Oh, it probably will. Or I might go and screw things up again. Who knows?" She took a deep sigh. "All I know is that I'm here at what's probably my favorite place on earth." She glanced across the cornfield on the north side of the property. "And I think I need to take some time to sort things out before I head west. This is the perfect place to do that."

David smiled and turned to get into his car. As he started the engine, Joani tapped on the passenger side window. He pressed the button to roll it down—this time, all the way down. "You really are welcome to come back." She seemed uncomfortable extending the offer. "I mean, I wouldn't mind seeing you again. Under calmer circumstances?"

"Maybe we can get together." He stumbled with his words, too. "I would like to see you again."

"OK, then. I'll be here." She pointed to the ground with both index fingers as she backed away from the car. "You know the way."

"Should I call first?" he asked, to be polite.

"Nah. You can't disturb a person sitting in a rocking chair unless you're tryin' to sell 'em something." She flashed an extremely attractive smile, and he drove down the drive toward the highway, and Springfield, and a life that had suddenly lost its boredom.

* * * * *

Snake did nothing to induce conversation on the trip back to St. Louis. He brooded on the passenger side, chain smoking cigarettes with long, slow, deep draws into his lungs. He flicked the butts out the window as the car trudged east on the interstate. Then he'd light another smoke as he pondered his situation.

The flunky, on the other hand, was in a talkative mood. "You get all your work done in Lebanon, Snake?"

"Yeah."

"I sure am glad I was home this evening so I could help you out. Glad my sister's car was available. She wasn't too happy about me takin' it on such short notice, but I told her . . . "

"I don't care about your sister. Just drive."

"Oh, sure. Sure, Snake." The flunky paused for at least a minute. "Say, you think that girl of yours is gone for good? Or you think she just freaked out and drove back to St. Louis?"

Snake seemed to stop and actually think about the question. "I got a feeling I know where she went. She's gonna regret this move when I catch up with her again."

"Ah, Snake, there's lots of girls out there. This one's trouble. I seen somethin' like this comin' for a while."

"You don't know nothin'. Just drive!"

The flunky continued his driving, passing slower cars as the sun started going down behind them in the western sky. "Say, Snake, you don't mind me sayin', but does that girl know much about your business? I mean, she wouldn't put the finger on you with the cops, would she?"

The idea startled Snake. He thought so much of himself, like he was indestructible. He was sure that he was clever enough and careful enough to never get caught at his illegal drug operations. However, this was the first time doubt, and even a little fear, had entered his mind. "She wouldn't dare. I'll kill her first."

"Nah, Snake, I don't think you oughta do that."

Snake whirled his angry, scraggily bearded face toward the flunky. Through his gritted teeth he muttered, "Just drive!"

SEVEN

David slept restlessly at the Super 8 motel in Springfield that night. He usually slept soundly. His normal routine on a business trip was to have a late snack, go over his notes for the next day, wash up, read a little, and then go to sleep. Tonight, his standard procedures were interrupted with thoughts about his unusual encounter with Joani Givens.

In the hour or so they were together, he saw a human metamorphosis. She changed from a savvy but frightened street-smart waif to a shy, pleasant, and enthusiastic young orphan woman. The farm seemed to change her attitude. Although she said she hadn't been at the farm physically in several years, the spirit of the open fields hadn't completely left her. And with one look at the summer homestead of her youth, her heart seemed to be rejuvenated and leap with joy and possibility.

There was no discounting the fact that she had broken

through David's mundane existence and touched something energetic and challenging in his soul. He really did want to see her again and discover more of the spirit that she exuded on that small family farm. *My dad said I would know when I was in love,* he thought. *Could this be the beginnings of what it feels like?*

This sense of reckless abandon was not a part of David's makeup. He lived by strict principles and a day-timer. He focused on proper sales techniques and regimentation. And yet this one auburn-haired, green-eyed escapee from the clutches of the seamy side of the big city had caused him to consider throwing caution to the wind. He was suddenly in the mood to run down a country road instead of using a stairmaster, to play in the mud instead of executing a perfect hook slide into second base, and to shout at the top of his lungs for all the world to hear: "Joani Givens, I think I might be falling in love with you!" During this brief encounter with her, he saw that Joani exhibited definite signs of a changed personality. He never dreamed that it was going to alter his life, too.

He finally fell asleep sometime after 2 a.m. and woke up at 7 a.m., an hour later than he normally did. He had eggs and bacon for breakfast instead of cereal and fruit.

His customers even noticed a change. One store owner asked, "What's gotten into you?"

"What do you mean?"

"Somethin' different about you today, David. You're usually pretty stiff and businesslike."

David steadied himself, not wanting to jeopardize his business relationship with this client. "I'm sorry. I'll try to straighten up."

"No, no," he replied. "I think it's great. My wife and I been a little worried about you. Like you take your work so serious that you forgot about the other hours in the day."

Even in Joplin, the store owner there ordered extra items.

He said he perceived a renewed sense of enthusiasm in David. "Ain't seen you this happy since the Cardinals made a serious run for the pennant," he said.

David drove on to Tulsa, then Oklahoma City, and went to a ballgame there as planned. The euphoria didn't subside. Even the game looked fresher. But instead of keeping score and staying to himself as he usually did when he went to a game alone, he wanted to strike up conversations with the people around him. He wanted to talk about baseball and sunsets and growing up on the farm and what it was like to fall in love. It couldn't have been simply the adventure of helping someone. It had to be that *someone* whom he had helped. David's dad always said he would know, and he was beginning to sense that his time had come. He even called his parents the next day.

*   *   *   *   *

"Hi, Mom. It's David. I'm in Oklahoma."

"David. You usually don't call 'til you get home from a trip. Anything wrong?"

"No, I just wanted to talk."

"OK," she said haltingly.

"I'm in Oklahoma."

"You already said that, Son."

"Did you see the sunset tonight, Mom?"

"Not really. Let me have you talk with your father."

Jack got on the phone. "Hi, David. How's business?"

"Hi, Dad. Business is good. Really good. I saw a great ballgame in Tulsa last night. No, Oklahoma City. You see that sunset tonight?"

"You feeling OK, David? You sound funny."

"Sure. I'm doing great."

"You haven't started drinking, have you?"

"No," he insisted. "I just wanted to call and talk."

"David, it's Mom again. Did you meet a girl?" The question brought on a clumsy pause in the conversation. "David, are you still there?"

"Yeah, Mom."

"'Yeah, Mom,' you're still there? Or 'yeah, Mom,' you met a girl?"

"Yeah to both of those questions." David heard his mom murmur "Praise the Lord" in whispered tones. Jack broke through the hush with a noticeable laugh in his voice.

"How'd you meet her?"

"That's a long story." *How am I ever going to explain the circumstances to them or anybody else?* he thought. "I'll have to sit down and tell you all about it when I see you next time. I'm hoping to see her again on Friday. She's living outside of Springfield."

Jack snickered. "I thought it was either love, or alcohol, or indigestion by the tone of your voice. Good luck, Son. Talk to you again soon. I'm in the middle of cleaning the garage and I want to get it done before the Cubs game tonight."

David heard the click of the extension phone in his mom and dad's garage. Mom was still on the line. "When are we going to meet this girl?"

"Meet her? I don't know, Mom. It's complicated, but interesting."

"I understand. I'll let you go. You don't need to spend all your money talking to me on the phone. Come see us. We'll talk then for free."

"OK, Mom. I love you."

"I love you, too, David."

David hung up the phone and flung himself back on the bed in his motel room. He couldn't believe he'd confessed to his parents that he might be in love. He didn't even know that for sure himself. However, there was no mistaking the fact that Joani had caused a noticeable change in his otherwise docile personality. And on Friday, he'd be able to swing through Fair Grove on his way back to St. Louis and see if this spell was still having its effect on him.

EIGHT

David went back to cereal and fruit the next morning. He was partial to cereal and fruit, and he had them nearly every day. It might be a boring breakfast, but he liked it.

He had two morning appointments in Joplin before heading back to St. Louis. *I should be able to make Fair Grove by early afternoon.* He didn't want to rush these clients in Joplin. After all, they were two of his most lucrative accounts. Love was one thing, but business was still very important to him.

David had a few vacation days coming to him. *Maybe Joani would want to go to Illinois with me and meet my parents. Wait, did I just say that? I can't believe I'm even thinking this way.* However, a hypnotic, intoxicating feeling of unbridled joy had swept through him like the wind after a fresh spring rain. He liked the feeling. It wasn't boring.

The first client took longer than expected. The second one

was preoccupied with a water pipe break, but he still needed to talk personally with David, taking more time than the appointment should have taken. He grabbed a bite to eat at a diner across the street from his store while the owner was handling his water problem. It was after 2 o'clock by the time they got together and took care of business. David didn't get out of Joplin until 3, and he knew it would take a good hour to drive to Fair Grove.

The reality of water pipes and tools and talking with clients had taken some of the joy out of his attitude. He felt like he was coming back down to earth after a hot air balloon ride. That feeling got stronger as he passed through Springfield and headed toward the Fair Grove exit off I-44 that had been a part of the uplifting change in his life a few days before. David was still excited about the possibilities that a trip to Aunt June's farm would hold, but he was also experiencing the normal fatigue of a road trip by now, and only wanted to get the drive over with so he could see Joani again.

David didn't drive over the speed limit. That was another one of his boring principles. He figured there was no sense in speeding and getting a ticket that would not only cost him money, but also jeopardize his driving record. David couldn't afford to have his license suspended or revoked with all the driving he had to do with his job. Besides, Missouri had passed a seventy mile-per-hour speed limit law that made the trips go faster anyway. He figured out that a driver wouldn't cut that much time off a three-hour drive by going eighty instead of seventy.

David's dad used to raise a major fuss when the highway speed limits were only fifty-five. He would constantly bark, "The government's telling us it's to conserve fuel, but I still smell a conspiracy in there somewhere." When David was a little kid, it seemed like Jack got at least one ticket every time the family drove from their home in Indiana to visit Grandpa

Norm at the farm in Mattoon.

David got so hypnotized by the drone of the road hum and his fatigue from this five-day trip that he almost missed the Fair Grove exit. He had to cut back over to the right lane after passing a slower car and then put on his signal quickly. He hated when drivers did that to him. *Never saw how they could be so indecisive or preoccupied. I guess now I know.*

David followed the same roads that Joani had led him down a few days before. Nothing changed much in this part of the country over the years, let alone the last couple of days. Farms stayed in family hands for generations. Sure, some of the kids got out of the business and moved to town to work at the Walmart. Or they might go to college and get a teaching job or sell insurance. Most of them moved back close to home even if they didn't want to farm for a living. There was always one or two of the offspring who would decide that farming was their chosen profession. They would stalwartly continue the family line and till the rich soil they grew up on.

And when families got together for Christmas holidays, they wouldn't go to the insurance salesman's house. They'd gather at the farm, where the memories flooded their souls. Where they laughed uproariously, ate overabundant meals around the big table and a couple of card tables in the living room, and watched the sunset like they'd done so many times in years past. And they'd laugh some more, open simple but thoughtful presents on the floor of the living room, eat some more, and sleep crowded into the beds and rooms that seemed so much bigger a few years ago when they were children.

That was a heritage David sought for himself and his future family. That was what he desired to pass on to future generations of Freemans. Maybe someday he could even move back to the Illinois farm of his youth and gather his children and grandchildren and explain to them what life was all about. David's wife baking biscuits that would send an intoxicating aroma wafting through the house and out the front door, where he would sit with their offspring in rocking chairs that creaked ever so slightly against the old wood of a front porch that looked out over simplicity and solemnity.

He turned right down the dirt road and looked for the farmhouse. "There it is," he said out loud, recalling Joani's excitement when she saw the old white structure on the horizon.

David pulled into the driveway and stopped at the top of the circle near the fence gate. "I wish I could have called first to let them know I was coming to visit, but I didn't have their number," he whispered. Besides, Joani and Aunt June had both invited him to come back. And he wasn't selling anything. He was calling on friends. A friend doesn't need a good reason to stop by and say hi.

He parked the car and got about halfway up the concrete walkway when Aunt June came out of the front door, again wiping her hands, as if now by natural habit, on her red and white plaid apron. It was like time stood still on the farm while David had done business for several days.

"Hello, Aunt June." He didn't know what else to call her. "It's David Freeman. I met you the other day when I dropped Joani off."

"Oh, David. Hello. I didn't recognize you at first. I gotta get new glasses someday." She stuck out her hand as David walked up the steps to the porch. "How are you? Did you have a good trip to . . . where was it you were going?"

"Springfield, Joplin, and then Oklahoma for a couple of days."

"My, you have been on the road. Sit down and rest. I'll get you some iced tea." She motioned for him to sit in one of the rockers. "You like lemon and sugar in your tea?"

"Yes, lemon and sugar would be fine. I, uh . . . I was wondering if Joani was around."

June had turned to go back in the house to get the tea, but

stopped and turned back toward David. "She's not here right now," she said with a hesitating tone. "She went into town a little while ago. She should be back soon. Sit down, David. I'll get the tea. Then, we'll talk." She scurried nervously back into the house, never raising her eyes to meet his.

David settled into the wooden seat and simultaneously heard and felt the natural wood creak of the chair. He was tired enough that he wanted to close his eyes, but on the other hand, he wanted to drink in the pastoral scenery of the farm.

June emerged with two glasses of iced tea. She handed David one and sat in the chair next to his. "My husband is in the barn tending to something. You didn't meet him the other day when you dropped Joani off, did you?"

"No, I didn't."

"Well, he should be back at the house in a while for supper. He always seems to know when supper's ready." Her face changed to an expression of concern. "I wanted to talk with you about Joani."

"Sure, what about?"

"How well do you know her?"

"Not well at all. I just met her the other day when I drove her out here."

"She grew up in a pretty tough environment. Her mother, my sister, had a good heart, but no luck or sense. She never liked the farm life. Always dreamed of goin' to the big city and takin' it all in. When our parents died just after Herb and I got married, we offered to take her in and have her live with us on the farm. She opted for a foster home. I think that had something to do with cultivating her restless spirit. She ran away from there several times. Lost track of her for a while. She'd headed for the city lights. When we finally got back in touch, she told us she'd had several jobs; none of them panned out. She didn't say much about what she did. She got married and had Joani right away. He didn't stay too long, so Joani never knew her dad. My sister did her best to raise Joani, but being a single mother twenty years ago was no easier than it is today. Herb and I offered to help. We took Joani for the summers after school was out. But Joani's mom seemed embarrassed to take much in the way of money or advice from Herb and I. She didn't even tell us she was sick. And then when she died, well, we were just heartbroken. She wasn't a bad person. She just had no direction."

David had learned more about Joani's upbringing in those few minutes than he had ever expected to learn on this trip.

"What I'm trying to say, Mr. Freeman . . . "

"Please, call me David."

"David, Joani's a lot like her mom - a good heart, but she's got troubles, too."

"I don't understand what you're trying to say to me."

A gruff voice came from the side of the house. "She's trying to say that Joani doesn't need some travelin' salesman to wreck her life any more'n it already is."

"Oh, Herb." June jumped from her chair and wiped her hands again on her apron. "David, this is my husband Herb."

Herb strolled around toward the front of the porch, never flinching in his nontrusting glare of David, who rose and climbed off the porch to meet him. He stuck out his hand to shake and hopefully break the ice, but it was cordial and formal, not like the handshake of someone who wanted to get to know you.

"Didn't mean to startle you," Herb said apologetically. "Couldn't help but overhear my wife goin' on about Joani. Truth is, the girl's got trouble."

June butted in. "I was trying to tell David that, Herb."

Herb shushed her with an abrupt motion of his hand. "Truth is, she's got no sense. Somebody like her, in her twenties already, should have more sense. She's been trouble for a while. Last four days she's been getting worse every day."

June bounded down the steps, holding on to the porch post. "She's got a problem with . . . alcohol."

"That's not the only problem she's got," Herb barked.

"She needs help. She needs some guidance in her life."

"She needs a swift kick," Herb snapped.

"Oh, Herb." June swatted Herb on the shoulder and turned back to David. "She talked about you the night you drove her here. She said you seemed like a nice, stable person."

"You never told me that," Herb interrupted.

June continued. "I sensed that about you, too, when I met you." Herb gave June a scrunched-face look like she had just told the used car dealer the sticker price was more than fair. She shrugged him off and pulled a step closer to David. "Joani started drinking the day after she got here, and I don't think she's stopped much." June paused to collect her thoughts. "She needs a friend, David. A stable friend. We try to talk to her, but we're family, and she thinks we don't know anything about life, living out here on the farm. We just don't know what to do with her."

Herb took the lead in a calmer, more patriarchal voice. "We want what's best for Joani. And drinkin' and carryin' on is not puttin' her in that direction. Maybe you could help. What do you sell?"

"I work for Jay Tools."

Herb paused before asserting, "Good products. Use 'em myself." He shook David's hand and then turned to walk toward the back door. Herb had said his mind.

June continued the conversation. "I'm not sure when Joani will be back. She left in a huff, a couple, three hours ago. You're welcome to stay for supper."

Herb turned from his walk to the back door. "Stay for supper. You're welcome here."

"Well, I guess I could."

June glanced over David's shoulder toward the driveway

and sighed, "Here she comes now." The plain green Chevy Tudor was kicking up dust as it weaved down the driveway.

Herb walked back when he saw the car approaching. "She thinks my car's an outdated piece of junk, but she has no trouble borrowing it."

June turned Herb around and pushed him toward the back door. "Herb, go get washed up for supper." Then she turned back to David. "Would you talk with her?"

"Sure," he said with a slight hesitation. The Joani Givens adventure was starting all over again.

David walked toward the car. Joani exited the Chevy and, when she recognized him, shouted, "Hey, Dave. You came back!" A cigarette hung from her mouth like a familiar appendage. Her auburn hair was ruffled and she staggered slightly as she walked around the front of the car toward him. He waited on the sidewalk as she approached carrying a small brown paper bag.

Joani put her left hand around his neck. "How's it goin', sport?" He could tell she'd been drinking, not savagely, but consistently. "You came back," she pouted.

"I . . . I don't know what to say."

"Don't say anything. Kiss me." Grabbing her cigarette with the same hand she was holding the paper bag, she pulled David's head quickly toward her with her other hand, planting a sloppy kiss on his lips. This was not the "first kiss" from Joani that he had fantasized about for the past few days. He pulled away, gripping her left hand and releasing the hold she had on his neck. "Guys like kissin' me. What's wrong with you?"

"What's wrong with me?" He was provoked by the unexpected situation that was developing. "When I left you the other day, you were different. You were happy to be out of the city, away from that Snake guy, and the farm seemed to bring out a *positive* joy and a life in you. What happened to you?"

She sauntered down the walk toward the front porch, taking a drag on her cigarette. "I guess it's Herb and June. They got nothing exciting to do around here." She turned back toward him. "They only got twelve channels on the TV. I'm bored, David. You ever been bored?"

"Sure." He walked toward her. "But I didn't go off the edge like you seem to be doing."

"What do you know? You meet me one time. I snooker you into driving me to my aunt and uncle's farm and you think you know me?"

David suddenly realized that he didn't know her at all. The auburn-haired green-eyed beauty that he had rescued days before had let her true personality shine through for him to clearly see. What a letdown! This was worse than losing a ballgame in the last inning on a stupid error. After a big loss, David's high school coach once said, "You guys should be lower than a snake's butt in a tractor rut." This was worse than that. This was the blues times ten.

Herb held open the front door and called out, "Joani, dinner."

Joani rolled her eyes. "OK, Herb." She walked toward David. "C'mon and stay for supper. At least we eat good around here." Why she wanted to pursue this any further was beyond David's comprehension.

He hesitated as she inched a step closer to him. "I don't think I should," he said. Any attraction he had toward her was fading fast.

She coyly took another step closer to him. "C'mon. We'll eat. We'll talk. We'll take a walk." Her eyes brightened. "Maybe you can drive us to Springfield," she said, excitedly.

"I don't think I should."

She stood straight up and put her hand on her hip. "David, wake up," she said with a stern look on her face. "Who'd you think I was when you met me? I was a waitress in a seedy little bar in St. Louis who was living with a drug dealer."

David looked around at the gentle surroundings of the farm. A light breeze blew against his face. The leaves in the big oak tree closest to them made a rustling sound. "I thought maybe the farm would have a reassuring effect on you. I thought maybe you were wanting to put your past behind you and start over."

"I wanna *live* my life," she said. "Nothing holding me down. Haven't you ever wanted to live like that?"

"I have principles that I live by." Those words sounded so pompous, and David regretted saying them, especially when Joani responded by laughing.

"Well, you must be the last principled man on earth, 'cause I've never known a guy who lived that way."

"And you probably never will," he blurted out, regretting he'd said that, too. It was obvious that his temper was getting in the way of his words and he wasn't expressing himself as clearly as he wanted to. They stood there in silence staring at each other for the longest of seconds. David finally broke the silence. "I gotta go." He turned toward his car.

"Don't," she begged.

He turned back toward her. "I gotta." He was frustrated that he wasn't saying anything that had the possibility of making something positive out of this situation. "You know, I really liked your spirit when we met the other day. But I think I mistook your wild side for an adventurous spirit. There's a difference."

"I'm really not that bad. I drink a little, but that's just to relieve the boredom."

"There's other ways to do that."

"Then stay, and let's talk about it," she said as if she really wanted him to. However, he couldn't think of one reason why he should.

David's fantasy of thinking he might be falling in love with her was being pushed abruptly out of his mind by her real character that she was revealing today, and that was so much different from his character. It was clear that their spirits were diametrically opposed. Opposites have been known to attract, but whatever it was that initially brought them together and held them together for a short while was losing its grip with each disappointing minute they stayed together.

"Some other time," he sighed.

"Promise?"

"Sure," he said, keeping the door open ever so slightly. Deep down, he really did want to stay. Perhaps there was a possibility that they could form a bond, but frankly he was confused. He had fantasized about their relationship for several days, and reality was a whole new ballgame. A relationship with Joani Givens was going to take a lot of work. And David wasn't sure if he was up to putting that much work into it. He glanced back at her as he opened the car door. "You take care of yourself."

She was still looking at him. "I got nothin' else to do."

She gave him a little wave and turned to walk toward the house. David started the car and glanced her way as she ambled down the path. She turned as he put the car into drive. He managed a quick wave of his hand toward her. She raised a disappointed hand in his direction, too.

He resigned himself to the fact that this would probably be the last time he'd ever see her. They were so different.

Sadly, a closer relationship didn't seem like it had the remotest possibility of working out.

NINE

David felt like someone close to him had died. He felt like he had died, while watching his dreams vanish in a flash fire of disappointment. He drove home to St. Louis in a stupor of disillusionment. His job meant nothing. His house meant nothing. A steady rain began to fall and dampened his spirits further. He pulled his car into the garage and went into his house not wishing to reenter the world for however long it took to escape this funk.

He turned the TV on by habit. The Cardinals game was rained out, of course. Atlanta was playing at San Diego and the game wouldn't start until ten o'clock. The Cubs played that afternoon. He couldn't even skip out on his troubles by watching a ballgame. He sorted his clothes from the trip, as usual, and put a load in the wash. He ordered a pizza, but didn't really feel like eating it.

"What was I thinking?" David moaned. "Real love, would have to be easier than this." It would take a lifetime of effort to navigate a path through Joani's heart's complex workings. Love should be more like the movies. It should be peaceful and tranquil like a summer day on the farm. It shouldn't be complicated—not this complicated.

He lay around and moped all day Saturday, not even getting dressed or going out. He stayed in his sweat pants and T-shirt all day. His appetite was nonexistent so he only snacked on cold day-old pizza. He mindlessly flipped through the TV channels and put on the occasional CD while halfheartedly working at little chores around the house. It's a shame to quit on love so soon, he thought. But it let me down bad. Or else I didn't really understand it to begin with.

He left the phone machine on all day and didn't listen to the messages until later that evening. Insurance salesman. The church reminding him about the voter's meeting after late service tomorrow. Another insurance salesman. Dunn and Bradstreet wanting to update his file. His mom. She wanted to know how he was doing. I hate to call her. I'm sure she'll want to know about "the girl."

David waited an hour after he checked his messages, debating with himself about avoiding the confrontation with his parents. "Oh, so what?" he finally reasoned out loud. "It's just a relationship that you never really had in the first place that's gone bad. Not like it hasn't happened to anyone else in the world before. This is what country music songs are based on." David's parents had always been understanding and supportive. "I'll give 'em a call," he reasoned.

It was nine o'clock in the evening. They were usually still up this time of night. Sylvia answered the phone. "Hello," she said in a groggy voice.

"Hi, Mom. It's David."

"David, hi. What time is it?"

"Did I wake you up?"

"No, I was dozing on the couch. Now, where is . . . where's your father?"

Jack had picked up the extension phone in the garage. "I'm out here in the garage."

"Are you still out there? When are you going to be finished with that project?" David laughed at the concept that he was listening to a conversation between his parents, who were two rooms apart.

"Hi, Dad."

"Hi, Son. How was your trip?"

"Good. I got back yesterday, but I've been kind of busy around the house."

"Me too," Jack replied. "I've been putting up some shelves here in the garage so we can organize and store some things."

Sylvia was the first to bring up David's "love life." "So how about that girl you met?"

David hesitated, but decided the best approach was simply to blurt it out. "I don't think it's going to work out, Mom."

"Oh, really," Sylvia responded in full "mom mode" as if she was trying to pat David on the head through the phone to console him.

"I just met her, and we're really different. I think she was carrying a lot of baggage that I couldn't handle."

"Is she a big girl?" Sylvia asked in a question that came completely out of left field. "No, no, that's not what I meant. Oh, I don't know what I meant. I think I'm still half asleep."

"That's OK, Mom," David assured her.

"Just . . . talk with your father. I'm going to crawl in bed."

"OK, Mom."

"Goodnight, David. Come see us sometime."

"OK, Mom. I will." He could hear her hang up the phone.

"Sorry about the girl, David," Jack said.

"Oh, it's OK. I think I got my hopes up too fast. Like I said, she had a little too much baggage for me to handle."

"We've all got baggage, Son."

"I know, Dad. But she had a lot. And I don't know if I could have handled it."

Jack stayed silent for a couple of seconds to measure his words. "Most of life is manageable and predictable, but love is always complicated."

"I guess you're right," David replied. "But it shouldn't be this complicated."

"When the right girl comes along . . . "

" . . . I'll know," David said, finishing his dad's sentence. "I know. You've told me that before."

"And it's still true."

"I guess so."

"Say, whatcha got goin' next weekend?" Jack knew it was time to change the subject. "I think I can get us a couple of good tickets to the Cubs game on Saturday afternoon against the Phillies. You interested?"

David hesitated only for a second because he needed to calculate his schedule. "Sure. I can make it."

"Can you come up Friday? Make a weekend of it?"

"Sure. I'll be there for supper. I wanted to take a day off work this next week, so no problem. I gotta leave on Sunday afternoon so I can be back for a Monday morning meeting."

"Great. We'll talk more then. Thanks for calling, Son."

"Thanks, Dad. See you next weekend."

David hung up the phone and realized as he had so many times in his life that he was blessed to have a wise and understanding father and a caring mother, too. He thought of Joani's upbringing and how awful her daily living environment must have been. No father around. A hooker for a mother. She did say her mother kept harping on her to make something of her life. *Too bad she didn't heed the warnings,* David thought. *Still, she had a lot to overcome. It's probably best that I put this inci-*

dent behind me. Chalk it up to experience, David, and move on. You're gonna see the Cubs next Saturday.

TEN

The drive to David's parent's home in Roselle, Illinois, a western suburb of Chicago, was about 300 miles from St. Louis and took a little more than five hours, or a leisurely six. It was highway all the way, without much traffic slowdown except in Springfield and Bloomington. However, it really slowed down in Chicago, depending on what time of day you arrived.

David always tried to plan the trip so he wasn't going through during rush hour. That often-used phrase is a misnomer anyway. Between four and six o'clock in the afternoon, no one is *rushing* in Chicago. The traffic slows to a stop several times during the commute. It should be called "rush-stop-rush hour." Everyone's trying to go faster than the driver next to them, but because there are too many cars and not enough roads that are not undergoing repairs, the traffic slows to a stop—often.

David did a lot of driving in city traffic in St. Louis, but he thought Chicago was different. The drivers seemed angrier. They darted in and out of traffic more than drivers did in other big cities. He once saw a cab driver get out of his car during a complete stop in traffic and punch another driver through his window for cutting him off earlier. *That's taking revenge a little far, in my opinion,* he thought.

David was not a violent person. He never had been. He was a fierce competitor when he played ball in high school and college, but he never got into any fights. The fight was more within himself than with any of his opponents. They were merely faceless people on the other side of the battle lines. The real battle was within. He felt like he had to do his best, and even when he failed, he tried to learn and grow so he could succeed the next time. The opponent had nothing to do with the process, except maybe to give him tips on how he might improve his game.

Jack and Sylvia moved to Roselle the summer after David's sophomore year in college. Since he grew up in Indiana and not in Roselle, he didn't have any high school friends to look up when he came back to town. Even if his folks still lived in Fort Wayne, only one of the "hossmen" still lived in town. The other two moved away like he did. And David considered it a sad reality that they didn't correspond much anymore except for an occasional letter or Christmas card.

He did like the Lutheran church his parents attended, although he didn't think he would when he first visited with them. *It's so huge. How is it possible that this big of a church can be the least bit friendly?* But he soon saw firsthand the principle that groups tend to go as leadership goes.

The pastor, Chuck Mueller, was a friendly, outgoing man in his early forties. He took over as head pastor when his father, Charles Sr., retired. They were both cut from the same amiable mold, but especially true to their respective generations.

Chuck related exceptionally well with his age group, but also branched out to touch others younger and older. He kept his sermons short and lively, relating stories that had something to do with everyday life instead of merely spouting academic-sounding theologies.

The music at Trinity was lively and offered a variety of styles that all ages could relate to. It took a while for David to get used to the more upbeat rhythms because he had grown up in a rather staid environment at his hometown church in Indiana. However, once he got to know several of the songs they used, he really enjoyed the enthusiasm and the joy that the new songs brought to the services.

I hope Dad won't want to play an early round of golf on Saturday morning, he thought. David didn't play golf very well, or often, just occasionally with a client who came to town. Besides, on Saturdays the courses are always busy with golfers who work during the week and are trying to squeeze in a "quick eighteen" between all their other weekend chores. *It's as slow as rush hour. How could a person possibly derive enjoyment from a game of golf on a crowded course when they've been fighting daily commuter traffic throughout the week!* He never saw the point of playing on the weekend.

* * * * *

The drive up to the western suburbs of Chicago went smoothly. David stopped once to get gas, use the bathroom, and get a bite to eat, all at one place. Now, as he approached the city on I-55, he noticed a gradual increase in the number of cars. Before the new 355/North-South Tollway was built, he had to take the Tri-State to 290 to get to Roselle. Or he could take a series of back roads like Joliet/Highway 53. However, he never knew which one of those roads was going to be slow. It could take forever darting from one road to another, hoping to find a quick route as he trekked north. The 355 is a straight shot with three or four lanes on each side. However, today, as David took the exit ramp for 355, he could see traffic was already backing up, and it was only two o'clock in the afternoon.

He waited patiently as the cars and trucks and motor homes inched along the ramp. He turned off the air conditioner and opened the windows, and a blast of hot Chicago mid-summer-like air hit him. *It's still spring,* he thought. *Summer's come early this year in Chicago.*

How could a city be so hot in the summer and so cold in the winter? With the traffic and the weather, it's no wonder a lot of these drivers seem mad all the time.

The traffic slowly started to pick up, and after about a mile of going 25-30 miles per hour, David could see why things had slowed down: an accident. Three cars had plowed into each other in the far right lane, probably a chain reaction when one car stopped suddenly. He glanced in his rearview mirror and saw flashing lights heading toward the scene. He passed the accident before the police could weave through the slow traffic. As he did, he noticed the drivers had gotten out of their cars and were talking. *Must not have been any serious injuries.* One of the drivers was a young, auburn-haired girl, reminding him of Joani. He hoped that his parents wouldn't bring up the subject, but he guessed it was inevitable.

Once the traffic passed the accident scene, the cars were all able to pick up speed. No tie-ups the rest of the way into Roselle.

David drove into the driveway of his folks' Roselle home, a modest ranch on a half-acre lot in a tree-spotted neighborhood with other middle class families. They had moved there when Jack got a job with a different company. David had figured his dad's job at his previous company was going to be phased out in a couple of years, so he made inquiries with his business contacts throughout the Midwest about some available options. The company did shut down completely, as David remembered, and Jack was one of the fortunate ones who had seen the light early and planned for the future. He got something steady in Roselle that paid even more than he was making in Indiana. Some of the others in his plant were left out in the cold. David surmised the problems were caused by poor management and shifting markets, but he never really talked about it with his dad. Both Jack and Sylvia seemed very happy living and working in Roselle.

David rolled into the driveway and no more shut off the car when his parents sprang out of the front door. "David. David. You're here!" his mom shouted for the neighborhood to hear. They both briskly covered the length of the front walk before the screen door had a chance to close behind them.

"How was the drive, Son?" Jack inquired.

"No problem."

"Wasn't it hot? It's so hot," Sylvia exclaimed.

"Nah, I sipped on some ice cold pop the whole way."

Jack opened the car door on the passenger side to help carry David's luggage in the house and noticed the small open ice cooler David usually carried along on trips. As he closed the lid, he asked, "Did you buy ice?"

"Yeah, I got a bag when I got the six pack of pop."

"You bought ice?" He turned to David's mom. "Momma, make a note we buy David an ice maker for Christmas this year. His freezer in his refrigerator at home obviously doesn't have one." He smiled with a smirk and glanced back at David.

"I've got an ice maker in my refrigerator," David noted with a hint of sarcasm in his voice.

"And you bought ice?" his dad replied.

"It's one of the few luxuries I afford myself, Dad."

"I sure hope I can afford to buy ice someday." They both smiled at the exchange.

"Have you got everything?" his mom inquired.

"I travel pretty light, Mom."

"Then come inside and rest up a while before dinner."

The three of them spent Friday night sitting around the living room talking about life and work and a spattering of politics. It was casual and relaxing. They had dessert in the living room around eight o'clock as they talked. Sylvia had made an apple pie, rich with cinnamon and brown sugar. They heated it up and put a couple scoops of vanilla ice cream on it; the melting cream mixed in with each delicious mouthful. It was the kind of dessert David liked to eat in a bowl with a spoon so he could savor every bite.

Jack said he was tired and wanted to read a little before going to sleep. "I want to be rested up for tomorrow," he said. "Cubs and Phillies! I snagged us a couple of good seats along the first base line for tomorrow's game. Let's plan on getting down there early to watch batting practice and infield. OK?"

David nodded his approval. "See you later, Dad."

"Night, Son."

David helped his mother clear the dessert dishes, but she insisted they leave them in the sink until morning. She kissed him goodnight on the cheek and she retired to her room with Jack.

David flipped through the channels on the television for a while, but he got bored quickly and decided he'd hit the sack early, too.

David's parents had a wall full of books in their living room. Jack had probably read most every one of them at one time or another. One of his favorite pastimes was to go to the bookstore in the mall and look through the dollar bin. He could always come up with a book that looked interesting or one that had lost its media appeal so quickly that the store was desperate to unload its unsold copies on customers. Jack was always there to scoop up those books. Hard to tell if he'd ever paid retail for a book.

He also got books at garage sales. Sylvia would browse for trinkets and Jack would look for books. David remembered some of the titles they still had on the shelves from when he was growing up. He had been glancing through the neatly arranged volumes for several minutes when Jack's voice startled him from behind. "See anything you like?" David jumped. Jack chuckled. "Didn't mean to scare you."

"I thought you went to bed."

"I did. But I finished this book and heard you still up so I thought I'd put it back on the shelf or see if you wanted to start reading it."

"What's it about?"

"It's by Bill McCartney. Ever heard of him?"

"The football coach, Bill McCartney?"

"Yeah. He got out of coaching and started a national men's ministry called Promise Keepers. This edition was written before he got out of coaching. I got it for a couple of bucks. He's put out a new edition. I'd like to get that, too."

"Gotta wait 'til it hits the bargain table first, eh?"

"You got it, although I might buy this one off the rack."

"Must be pretty good for you to pay retail."

"Well, I've read a couple things from Promise Keepers and I like what they have to say. They talk about men being men of God instead of men of the world. Men praying and studying God's word. Bein' better husbands and better fathers. I went to a local Promise Keepers rally with some guys from church. It was really good. You oughta go sometime, too."

"I don't know if we've got that in St. Louis. At least I haven't heard about it at my church."

"Lots of Lutheran churches aren't too happy with Promise Keepers. Claim their doctrine doesn't harmonize just right with strict Lutheran doctrine. I suppose if somebody looked hard enough they could find a few things that don't match up exactly, but I can't see the harm in a bunch of men getting together and trying to find out how to be better husbands and fathers. Seems like we could use more of that."

"Yeah, I guess so."

Jack's face lit up. "The music at this rally was great. A couple thousand guys singing loud. It was really great."

"Sounds good."

"David, they've got some big rallies coming up in the next few months. I'm going to one in Indianapolis with a group from church. You ought to meet us there."

David hesitated. "Oh, I'd have to check my schedule. I took a day off this week. I may have to make up some time."

"Well, suit yourself." Jack started to put the McCartney book back on the shelf, but then handed it to David. "Give it some thought. I'm off to bed. See you in the morning, Son. Cubs and Phillies." He smiled and patted David on the back.

"Night, Dad," David said as he glanced at the book, *From Ashes to Glory*. He took the book with him to his room. He looked through it, stopping at the pictures, but he was more tired than he realized. *I'll start reading it tomorrow, maybe.* He put the book on the nightstand, turned off the light, and closed his eyes as he snuggled in under the covers. It was good to be home.

David slept in more than he had wanted to for a Saturday morning. His folks had probably both been up for a while. He staggered down the hall and into the kitchen. Sylvia was cleaning up the kitchen sink. She noticed David when he came around the corner. "Hi, sleepyhead."

"What time is it? I must have overslept."

"It's almost ten o'clock. You must have been really tired from your trip. You didn't stay up too late watching TV last night, did you?"

"No. I went to bed not long after you guys did. You sure it's ten o'clock?"

Jack came in from the garage. "Hey, sport. Stay up late readin' last night?"

"No, but I must've been more tired than I thought."

Mom ushered David into a chair at the kitchen table as he continued to wipe the sleep from his eyes. "You want some breakfast, or lunch, or brunch?"

"Just let me wake up first, Mom. I'll be all right in a minute."

"I did my workout already this morning, David. Thirty minutes on the bicycle," Jack proclaimed proudly.

"Then he went and took a shower and laid down for another thirty minutes," Sylvia chimed in.

Jack smiled. "My body ain't as young as it used to be. My mind is still chasin' flyballs in an outfield somewhere, but my legs have trouble gettin' me to the end of the backyard."

David was concerned about Jack's health. "You're not having any serious trouble health-wise, are you?"

"No, I'm gettin' old."

"Jack, you're as old as you feel," Sylvia said.

"Yeah, well, some days I feel pretty old," he joked. "Actually, I'm feelin' pretty good today. C'mon, let's get goin'. Get something to eat. Get ready. We got tickets to that Cubs game."

ELEVEN

Jack and David drove toward Lake Michigan, where Wrigley Field has been a revered landmark on the Chicago North side since 1914. It had managed to keep the charm of an old ballpark while other teams had built concrete coliseums and domed carpeted palaces. Wrigley was more like old Ebbets Field in Brooklyn, Crosley Field in Cincinnati, or Tiger Stadium in Detroit. All three of those parks are gone now, but Wrigley stands as a monument to the best days of baseball, before salary arbitration and playing on artificial turf.

Wrigley seats less than 40,000, and the ticket prices are somewhat reasonable compared to other parks, so they don't have much salary money to throw at superstars. Through it all, the Cubs still managed to draw good crowds of loyal fans to the ballpark or to their TV sets to watch the games on cable.

There is a wind that blows in off the lake a few blocks from the ballpark. Some days you don't know if you should wear short sleeves or a winter coat. It depends on which direction the wind is blowing. Some days your comfort depends on whether you sit in the shade or the sun. The bleachers always provide excitement for rowdy fans, but David didn't really like to sit out there because he preferred to be a little closer to the infield action.

Going to a Cubs game as a father and son is a doubly grand experience.

Jack and David had begun a tradition when they first started going to Cubs games of driving around the ballpark before finding a parking spot. "Did I ever tell you about the time I almost caught a batting practice home run while driving around the park?" Jack said.

"No, what happened?"

"I was doing this—driving here on Waveland Avenue. These guys were standing out here trying to catch homeruns that came over left field during batting practice." He pointed to the young guys on the right side of the street, mostly teenagers and twenty-year-olds with some little kids mixed in. "One guy started walking in front of my car looking toward the field and bringing his glove up in the air. I slammed on the brakes and he looked my way. I just missed bumping him. He looked back to the field and I glanced that way also and saw a fly ball hit the very top of the outfield fence right up there." He pointed to the chain link fence attached high on the brick wall. "If that thing would have gone over, I swear I could have caught it sitting right here in the driver's seat. That is, if that guy hadn't jumped over my hood and made a diving catch with his glove." They both laughed at the possibility. "I wonder how many guys do get hit by cars along here just for the chance to catch a major league baseball."

"If ya gotta go, that might be the way to go," David said, smiling.

The crowd was filing toward the gates. Folks were buying tickets at the counters. Cars were finding their way to the various parking lots in the neighborhood around the field. It looked like it was going to be a beautiful, sunny day at the ballpark many people call the "Friendly Confines."

Jack found a parking lot a couple blocks away, down a side street, and it only cost him twenty dollars; he felt lucky, aware of how much parking was jacked up by the mini-entrepreneurs around the park. "Not too bad, although getting home might take a while," he said, aware of all the impending traffic and narrow side streets. Both men carried their light jackets as they approached the Wrigley entrance.

At the top of the fourth inning as the Phillies were coming to bat, Jack was munching on his popcorn and out of the blue turned to David and asked, "So, what about this girl you mentioned a couple weeks ago?" He caught David off guard. There was a pause before he added, "It's not that *I* want to know. Your *mother's* been concerned." Jack smiled a sheepish grin and then stuffed several kernels of popcorn into his mouth.

David drew a deep breath and prepared to tell the long version of the Joani Givens story, but thought better of it and simply blurted out, "She's a girl I met. She was pretty and had a nice smile, and I thought I liked her, but I got the feeling quickly that it wasn't going to work out. That's all."

"What was wrong with her?"

"Nothing. Well, actually, a lot of things."

Jack smiled. "Which is it?"

The batter digs in. Here's the pitch. He grounds to second for the first out in the Phillies half of the fourth.

As they watched the play and the cheers from the crowd died down, David leaned toward Jack and continued, "I think I imagined too soon that she was special. But then when I got to know her a little bit more, I saw that she had a lot of baggage from her past." Jack was silent on purpose so David could put the finishing touches on his thoughts. "It looked like it was going to be too much of a hassle to work through."

"Too much of a challenge?"

"Yeah, I guess so."

"Since when did you start backing down from challenges?" Jack quietly remarked.

His comment caught David by surprise. He paused to think how he could rephrase his thoughts to better explain the situation with Joani. "I just found out really quickly that we were two different people, from different backgrounds, with different lifestyles. I misjudged her when I first met her, and I'm actually glad I found out early that it wouldn't have worked out."

Jack turned forward to watch the game and ponder his own thoughts. He crunched another kernel of popcorn. "Maybe so," he posed, "but since when did you start backing down from a challenge . . . " he paused and turned to David, " . . . so quickly."

Second batter for the Phillies. Pitcher takes the sign and delivers. A curve ball. Easy tapper back to the mound, and a second out. But here comes the Phillies' big slugger, and the crowd starts to buzz.

"I sized up the situation early and thought that it just wouldn't work out. That's all." David was starting to get a little ticked off at his old man; however, the smile that came over Jack's face calmed him down.

"David, I noticed a tone in your voice when you said 'she was pretty and had a nice smile.' It was a 'boy, I wish this could have worked out' tone. I haven't heard that in your voice for a few years. Not since that what's-her-name girl you dated in college."

"I guess so, Dad."

The slugger digs in; the tension builds. The Cubs pitcher carefully looks for his catcher's sign. The pitch—and a long, long drive . . . but curving foul. The crowd breathes a collective sigh of relief.

"I don't know, David. Maybe I'm reading the situation wrong, but it sounds a little like you're brushing her off really quickly, but deep down you're not sure if that's the right thing to do."

"It would have been too big of a challenge." David was now repeating himself due to his dad's perseverance, but he pondered the thought that maybe his dad was right.

"David, you've always been a stand-up guy. You've been in tough situations and you've met them head-on."

Pitcher throws an off-speed curve ball, and the Phillie's slugger doesn't offer on it. Ball one, strike one.

Jack continued. "You remember the incident with Mrs. Rantoul?" What a memory flood that brought up for David.

The infamous "Mrs. Rantoul incident," as it became known, actually started with *Mr.* Rantoul. David was nineteen and his whole summer was baseball. He coached in a daytime league for kids eight through fifteen years of age and played on a Stan Musial League team in Fort Wayne. On the nights when he wasn't playing ball, he umpired the local little league and pony league games to make a couple of extra bucks. They didn't even have umpire uniforms. Instead, they wore T-shirts and shorts. And David's home plate gear was some old catcher's equipment he still had.

The pitcher eyes the plate. He delivers a fastball that is fouled straight back to the backstop by the Phillie's hitter. He's keying in on the Cubs' pitcher and everyone knows it.

The pony league games were usually hotly contested. David liked it that way, but he was aware that as the action heated up, the umpires could occasionally be the focus of the fierceness. Nothing too dramatic usually. Some catcalls and the occasional coach coming out to argue a play that didn't go their way.

The game in question with Mr. Rantoul's team was going

along normally until the bottom of the sixth inning. David was the umpire in the field, although he had brought his plate equipment along with him and stored it near the backstop rather than take it back out to his car in the parking lot before the game.

Mr. Rantoul's team was down two runs and David made a call on an overthrow that brought in two runs and caused the coach to go ballistic! He came running out onto the field right at David, waving his arms and shouting. Before he could even get to him, David made the motion that Rantoul was out of the game, but the coach continued to argue profusely. There was a lot of noise coming from players and fans, but most of it was coming from Rantoul himself. "I've never seen a call like that! How could you call that?"

David tried to explain the ruling, but the coach didn't want to listen. David's umpiring partner, an older adult, closer to Rantoul's age, stepped in to calm the situation. He told Rantoul that the play stood and he was going to have to leave because he'd been ejected from the game. That started things up all over again.

Here's a fastball that tails in high and tight on the Phillie's slugger who is really hugging that plate. It's two-and-two and, it's clear these two are in a battle.

"What do you mean I'm ejected from the game?" Rantoul yelled as he flailed his arms like an angry goose raising its wings as it attacks an enemy. David's partner tried to calm him down again as Rantoul pointed at David and barked, "How can I get thrown out of a game for a mistake that this kid made?" It was a tense situation and David tried to keep his cool, but his blood was starting to boil. His partner told the coach once again that the play would stand and ushered Rantoul toward the sidelines.

The next batter hit a lazy pop fly for the third out of the inning. Rantoul's team was down four coming up to bat in their half of the seventh and what could be the final inning of the game.

Here's the pitch. Another foul ball down the left field line. The crowd is really getting into this confrontation between the Cub's pitcher and the Phillie's slugger. They are hanging on every pitch.

Rantoul's team went quietly in the seventh inning and the game was over. David started to head toward the parking lot out behind the outfield, but he remembered he had left his plate gear near the backstop. He knew he had to walk in front of Rantoul's bench and near the stands where the fans and the parents were sitting, so he took a deep breath and jogged toward the backstop.

The pitch. It's a slow bouncer down the third baseline, rolling foul. You can hear the Cub fans groaning. They thought the pitcher might have fooled him with that pitch.

No one said anything out loud so David could hear, but he caught some muffled grumbling. He avoided eye contact and gathered his equipment quickly and headed back out onto the field and toward the parking lot. He had almost reached the outfield grass when he heard Rantoul yelling at the top of his lungs, loud enough for David to hear: "I wish we could get some *good* umpires to do these games! Why do we have to have these kids who don't know the rules do our games? The umpire blew that game for us tonight!"

David knew he was only trying to egg him on. He knew he should have walked to his car and ignored him, but then Rantoul said the wrong thing altogether. "This guy tonight doesn't know *beans* about baseball!"

That did it. David threw down his equipment and headed back toward the bench. Rantoul obliged and headed in David's direction. David knew he wasn't going to come to blows with the coach. That didn't even enter his mind. However, he was going to let him have it verbally.

"You're the one who doesn't know the rules!" David shouted as they got closer to each other and a crowd of kids and adults gathered around them.

"How come I get thrown out of a game for a mistake that *you* made?" Rantoul bellowed.

"I didn't make a mistake, and you got ejected because you came running across the diamond like a bloomin' idiot! You were gone before you reached the mound, coach."

Cooler heads prevailed. Several adults saw that this argument was not going to go anywhere good, so they ushered the two in opposite directions, saying, "OK, guys, enough's enough."

This is where it became the *Mrs.* Rantoul incident.

As David turned to bend over and pick up his equipment, Mrs. Rantoul grabbed the front of David's shirt and held on. She looked him in the eye and tersely said, "I want you to apologize to my husband for calling him a blooming idiot." The situation had now become absurdly funny. David took it on himself to help her release her firm hold on his shirt, which was now getting quite wrinkled.

"Geez, lady," he said. "Get off me."

Several of the kids David coached during the day were at that game and witnessed the event. The next day he caught it from them as they spread the word. "Hey, Coachie, quite a show last night. Mrs. Rantoul didn't hurt you or anything, did she? I thought she was gonna pop ya."

Jack and David talked about the event that night after the game. Jack said he was proud of David for standing his ground. He said it would be a good life lesson he could look back on positively someday. However, the story didn't quite end there.

The Cub fans are on the edge of their seats as the duel continues. The pitcher knows he has to mix up his pitches. Here's a slider, and it's another foul ball down the left field line. The count is still two-and-two.

Late the next afternoon, right before supper, David got a

call from his umpiring supervisor. Of course, he had heard about the "incident" from the night before, and he assured David that he had made the right call. He was calling to tell David he had a cancellation and wanted him to umpire that night's pony league game. "You'll be behind the plate, David."

"Who's playing?" David asked.

"It's Mr. Rantoul's team. But don't let that bother you," he added quickly. "You can do it." David wanted to back out, but his supervisor hung up before he could. David told his mom that he had a game to umpire and headed out to the field.

The pitcher checks the sign from his catcher. He shakes it off. He shakes off another. He shakes off another. The batter calls "time," and backs out of the box. The fans are jeering this move by the Phillies batter, but it's a mix of nervousness and confidence on their part.

David took a deep breath before he got out of his car at the ball field. "Lord, help me get through this," he prayed. He gathered up his equipment and headed toward the diamond.

He took a little flack when he first arrived, but nothing serious. As the game went on, the comments from the crowd came fast and furious, but David didn't respond. Everyone sensed the awkward tension, but the game ended without incident.

David walked toward his car alone. He had answered the challenge with class and he was proud of it, but the situation had an overwhelming effect on him. Tears started welling up by the time he reached his car.

He didn't notice at first, but one of his daytime ball players had approached him from behind. It was Scotty Eagleson, a wisecracking but good-natured eleven-year old. He patted David on the back and was ready to say something smart when David turned and looked him in the eye. Scotty saw David's tears and realized how much the experience had affected him. Instead of tossing out a cute remark, he reached out and shook David's hand. "Ya did good, Coachie. Ya did good."

David smiled and said, "Thanks."

The crowd is on its feet. The Cubs pitcher winds up and throws a slider low and inside. The batter swings and misses. Strike three! You can hear the fan reaction. That's out number three. The inning is over. The slugger turns and breaks his bat over his knee. The crowd cheers as the Cubs leave the field, everyone congratulating the Cub pitcher on their way into the dugout.

Jack and David were on their feet applauding. Jack turned to his son and said, "The pitcher really answered the challenge there, didn't he?"

"He sure did," David said.

The Cubs won the game. They squeaked it out by scoring two in the bottom of the eighth and holding the Phillies off in the top of the ninth to win 5-4. It was a great game! David and his dad felt it deep in their souls: baseball is such a great game. What could be better on a sunny Saturday afternoon? David and his dad together at a ballgame, and the Cubs win.

They walked to the parking lot with the throng of happy, faithful fans. One diehard wearing a blue Cubs batting helmet commented along the way, "Ya gotta love seein' da Cubbies pull one out like dat." Another fan answered, "Yeah, it's a rarity."

The guys had to sit for a while in their car while the postgame traffic inched along. They listened to the game wrap-up on the radio, but David was also up for asking his Dad what he thought he should do about Joani. *Was I really backing down from a challenge, like he suggested? Just playing it lazy? Or was I smart in letting my relationship with the "wild child" go by the wayside?* These were the questions in David's mind as he reopened this tough topic with his dad.

"Dad, I'm curious about what you meant about me not being up for a challenge. You mean that?"

"I didn't mean it as a put-down, David. You're the one who

has to determine if this situation is worth the effort. Frankly, I think you should spend some time praying about it."

"Praying about it?" David knew his dad was a religious man. He was faithful in church. He wouldn't back away from a conversation about God. But he wasn't the kind of man who wore his religion on his sleeve and challenged everyone to try and knock it off.

"Sure. Pray about it. My pastor once said, 'How do you expect to find an answer to that problem you're having unless you get some bruises on your knees?'"

"I don't think I understand."

Jack took a deep breath. "What's the *right* thing to do, David? Isn't that the question you need to ask here? Just, what is the right thing to do?"

"It seems like the right thing for me to do would be to let it slide."

"OK, but what do you think God wants you to do?"

That question threw David for a loop. "How am I going to know what God wants me to do?"

"You pray about it," he said.

"Pray about it?"

"Yes. Pray about it."

"You think if I pray about it that I'll start hearing voices from heaven?"

"I doubt it. But if you do, listen, and do what the voice says. You saw *Field of Dreams,* didn't you?" They both laughed at that one, his dad's reference to the baseball movie about a farmer who listened to voices he heard—and followed his dream.

"Maybe I'll try it."

After they got home, they spent the evening half watching television and half talking about old times. David turned in fairly early and thumbed through the Bill McCartney book some more. He couldn't help but notice the struggles that

Coach McCartney went through when he was the head football coach at the University of Colorado. They were the kinds of stories that don't get included in the press releases. People generally consider a man fortunate to have such a prestigious position as head coach at a major university. However, when David saw the hassles McCartney had to face, he wondered whether it was worth it in the end for the coach.

His book constantly related that through all the trials he faced, McCartney relied on God to give him the strength to endure. David guessed that was a good lesson for him to learn, particularly in whatever he would decide about Joani.

He put the book on the floor next to his bed and turned out the nightstand light. As he lay there, David folded his hands over his chest and closed his eyes. He thought, *Maybe God will tell me what to do.* "OK, Lord, I'm asking," David quietly said out loud. "What do You want me to do about Joani? There, I said it. How about an answer?" It had been a while since David said his prayers before going to bed.

David didn't really expect God to immediately send him an answer to his prayer. He figured he'd probably have to ask Him a few times before He'd let him know what to do. "What do You want me to do, Lord? What do You want me to do?" Although he kept asking that one question and that one question only, he really did feel like he was talking with God instead of simply mulling over his own ideas in his own head. "What do You want me to do?"

David's mind went back to when he was a kid. Sunday school. Confirmation class. He never got involved in youth group activities at his church because he was too busy with high school sports. He did remember the pastor made the students memorize Bible verses in confirmation class. The "thees" and "thous" always messed David up, but he was still pretty good at memorization. Let's see: *"For God so loveth the world, that He gaveth His only begotten Son, that whosoever believeth in Him, shall not perish, but hath eternal life." I re-member that one!*

David turned and settled in on his side, happy in the thought that he had at least asked God to show him what to do. He grabbed the overstuffed pillow with both of his hands and dug his face into the soft foam and the cool cotton pillow-case. A feeling of genuine contentment came over him as he asked once more, "What do you want me to do, Lord?"

While he was resting, a strangely clear thought hit David: *If anyone is in Christ, he is a new creation. The old has passed away. The new has come.*

Where did that come from? he wondered. *Confirmation class? Haven't heard that one for a while.*

David faded into sleep with the thought of "What do You want me to do?" still wandering around in his head.

TWELVE

Because of his work schedule, David was an early riser. He set his alarm clock every day, but he usually got up before it went off. He used it as a last resort if he should sleep in for some reason. The Sunday morning sun came through the bedroom window at his parent's home with a silent flash across his face, and he was awake and squinting quickly. He had forgotten to twist-close the blinds the night before.

David could smell the aroma of his mom cooking bacon for breakfast. The family planned to go to Chuck Mueller's Bible class and then church. Since Sylvia wouldn't have a chance to fix a big lunch because David was heading back to St. Louis after church, she decided to go all out for breakfast. *There's nothing like a "mom" breakfast*, David thought.

David didn't think much about the early morning meal, except that experts had said it was the most important meal of the day. Most mornings, he ate his healthy and boring cereal and fruit, and he saved a more gourmet meal for evening dinner.

He did love going out to eat with friends or friendly clients. If he had to host a business dinner with an obnoxious or drunken client, he considered it a "part of the job" evening. His boss could tell when he had decided he was not going to enjoy the evening by what food he ordered. If David wanted to get out of there quickly, he'd order something light and simple, no appetizers. If he wanted to make an evening of it, he'd go the whole route: appetizers, soup, salad, steak or prime rib, and maybe even dessert. Then coffee for sure. Coffee was a dead giveaway that David was expecting to make an evening of it. He didn't normally drink it at home, at the office, or on the road. However, it always topped off the end of a good meal when he was spending a long evening with people whose company he enjoyed.

David stretched his arms and legs before heading out to the kitchen to check in with his mom and dad. The walk down the hall at his parents' home was a memory jogger with all the pictures of the family hung on the walls. Snapshots of past victories: uniformed players before and after games, posed and natural; confirmation and graduation, posed with gowns on, and more natural shots without gowns. David thought his formal high school graduation picture looked so stoic and serious, like he was frightened and bored. *I think I had mononucleosis at the time,* he thought.

Then, there were the collages. Sylvia would gather together fifteen to twenty snapshots they took over the years from various periods of family history, and position them in large frames. The athletic collage. The Christmas collage. The farm collage. That was the one David liked the most. Grandpa Norm with his firm jaw and bright eyes. Jack and David on a combine or eating Grandma's apple pie. These pictures, this hall—they were like gates that opened up to the best days of David's life—the eras he treasured the most.

He entered the kitchen into the bright Sunday sunshine, rubbing sleep and memories from his eyes.

"Hi, Mom."

"Good morning, David. You sleep well?" his mom asked in what other folks call a cheery Sunday morning voice, but one that was consistent with her personality throughout the week as well.

"'Course I did. I've got a guilt-free conscience," he replied.

"Oh, that's good. Keep it that way."

"Hi, Son." Jack walked around the corner of the hallway from his and Mom's bedroom side of the house.

"Doin' good?" David queried.

"Doin' great!" he exclaimed. "Look at how much weight I've lost." He unbuckled his belt on his pants. "My belt's on the last loop. A year ago I had it on the first one." He slid his pants around his waist and hips. "Loose as a goose."

"Not bad," David replied.

"Not bad? These are forty-sixes."

Sylvia chimed in. "When you can slide forties around like that, you'll have something to crow about."

"Watch me. The day I slide forty-inch-waist pants around like this, I'll either be ecstatic—or very sick."

All three laughed out loud, with Jack leading the charge. "You do look like you've lost some weight," David said. "How'd you do it?"

"I got back into exercising," he boasted.

"You said that yesterday. What've you been doing?"

"I got a used stationary bike from that secondhand sporting goods place in town. People buy sports equipment at full price, never use it, and sell it to these guys. They sell it to other folks, who never use it and sell it back to them again. The place should be called Vicious Cycles." That got them all laughing again.

"You're not going to sell yours, are you?" David asked.

"Not with results like this!" He twisted his waistband over his hips again.

"Dad's been at it for almost a year now," Sylvia gushed. "He's really consistent at doing his workout. I'm so proud of him."

"If your mother wasn't such a good cook, I'd have been back to a thirty-eight-inch waistline by now." He reached his arm around Sylvia's waist and kissed her on the cheek as he pulled her close.

Mom rolled her eyes. "Oh, my. I suppose when you do get to a thirty-eight-inch waist, you think you'll be able to chase me around the house?"

"Not a bad idea, Momma." Jack put both arms around her and kissed her on the lips. It was a joy for David to see his mom and dad so affectionate and playful with each other after all the years they had been married.

"Not in front of the boy," Sylvia joked.

"He's got to learn from somewhere." Jack hugged her tight and turned to David, giving him a wink.

"It's Sunday, Jack. Be good," David's mom scolded. "What kind of eggs do you want?"

"Scrambled's fine," Jack said.

"Scrambled's good for me too, Mom. No, wait, how about over easy? I can never make over easy eggs like you. Whenever I make eggs for breakfast, it seems like if I want scrambled, I could throw the eggs through a maze of razor blades and the yokes wouldn't break. But if I feel like over easy, I just have to look at the yoke wrong and it breaks. How do you do it, Mom?"

"Oh, it's practice, I guess."

"It's a mom thing," Jack chimed in. "There's no one like your mother, David. No one."

They finished breakfast and drove to church, arriving as

the early service was letting out.

Jack and Sylvia said hello to several people and introduced David to them. For a large church, everyone seemed fairly friendly. That was one of the consistent characteristics that David noticed about this church the first couple of times he went to services with his parents.

Reverend Mueller, "Pastor Chuck" to most of the flock, was greeting the last stragglers who were leaving. Many of the early service people had headed down the hall to the education wing to drop their children off at Sunday School classes and grab a cup of coffee in the fellowship hall before adult Bible classes started. Chuck noticed Jack, Sylvia, and David and turned to shake Jack's hand. "You folks comin' or goin'?" he said with a big smile.

"We're comin' in," Jack remarked. "There's always a couple of fish who don't flow with the rest of the school. Chuck, you know my son, David, don't you?"

Chuck shook David's hand vigorously as he said, "Sure! David, good to see you."

"Thanks, Pastor. Good to see you, too."

"You still in St. Louis?"

"Yes, sir. St. Louis."

"You go to John Brunette's church?"

"Yes, Pastor Brunette. You know him?"

"Sure. He's a great guy. You still sellin' tools?"

"Jay Tools. The best."

"Spoken like a company man. I want to hear how you're doing, David. Come with me while I get out of this robe." He turned to Jack and Sylvia. "You don't mind, do you? I don't get much of a chance to talk with David."

Jack chimed in. "Go ahead, you guys. Mom and I will go get a cup of coffee and save you a seat at the Bible study. OK?"

Chuck and David walked briskly toward the pastor's study off the side of the sanctuary. Chuck was an energetic, fast walker, so David had to pick up his pace to keep up with him.

"How's everything been going, David? You just up for the weekend to see your mom and dad?"

"Yeah. Dad got tickets to the Cubs game yesterday."

Chuck interrupted. "Wasn't that a great game! I caught the last part on TV. They really pulled that one out."

"Sure did. Getting to see the Cubs win anytime is great."

"You played ball in college, didn't you?"

"Oh, small college. I wasn't that good."

"That's not what your dad told me. He said you really hustled out there and gave it all you had all the time."

"Dad said that? Wow, that's pretty cool."

They got to the pastor's study and Chuck walked in and began taking off his vestments and white robe. "I've really had a great time getting to know your dad. Your mom, too, but especially your dad. We've had some great talks. He's quite a guy. You should be really proud of him."

"Oh, I am. He and my grandfather have been the two most influential people in my life. They're both really honest men who tell it like it is."

"Your dad really impressed me with the way he handled that job situation of his."

David hadn't thought that his dad's job change was that big of a deal. He reasoned he had merely seen the handwriting on the wall, that the company was on its way down, and that he better get out while the gettin' was good. "Well, yeah, businesswise, I'm glad he saw what was coming and found something else."

Chuck stopped for a second and stared at David. "Do you know all the circumstances about your dad's job change?"

"Just that the company was going under and Dad wanted to get something else while he could."

Chuck hesitated to measure his words. "Maybe you better talk with him some more about this. There's a lot more details to the story. It's really pretty remarkable."

"I don't understand."

"Well, I should let him tell you, but the gist of the story is that a couple of his bosses were coaxing him into doing some illegal activities, and your dad stood up to them and said he wouldn't do it."

"Illegal activities?"

"I'm not privy to all the details, but since he wasn't going to go along with them, they tried to make things tough for him, even make it seem like some of the shenanigans that were going on were *his* ideas. He had to cover his bases pretty good."

David must have looked confused. He stuttered, "I . . . I guess we never really talked about it. I was in college at the time. He didn't let on like it was too big of a deal. Just that he got a new job through some business contacts here in Roselle."

"That's when he and your mom started going here. And that's when we got to talking about what he should do. Sometimes we would sit and pray and ask God for His direction for the good part of an hour or so. He turned the whole situation over to God, and God led him through it. He was also fortunate that he had taken extremely detailed notes and found several witnesses to back him up. We used an attorney from here at the church to set the record straight."

"An attorney? I've never heard anything about this."

"I'm sorry to spring all this on you, David. I'm just so encouraged by your dad's faith during this time. He really showed some conviction."

David sighed confidently. "Well, I've always known my dad was a man of principle."

Chuck pointed at David. "*You* need to hear my sermon today."

"I do?"

"Yeah, this is exactly what I'm preaching about today." Chuck hung his robe up on a hanger in the closet. "See, your dad is typical of a man the world would call a man of principles, but I think he's a man of convictions."

"Aren't they the same?"

"Not at all. Principles, for the most part, are man-made. God gives us convictions. Come on. Let's walk to the fellowship hall." Chuck grabbed his zippered brown leather case that contained his Bible and started walking out the door. "You see, a thief can have principles. He may decide that he won't rob someone during the day because he might get recognized easier. Or he won't use a gun to rob someone because he knows if he gets caught he'll get more time in jail for using a weapon. However, the thief has not been *convicted* that stealing is wrong. See what I mean?"

"I guess I do."

People made cordial gestures toward Chuck as the two of them walked down the hall of the education wing. He answered every one, but kept focused on his conversation with David. "We need to be men of conviction, David. God's people need to live by what *He says* is right and not by what *we think* is right. And the only way to get to know what He thinks is right is to get to know *Him*."

They got to the double doors of the huge fellowship hall. A couple hundred people were standing and engaging in casual conversation and sitting at the cafeteria-style tables, most drinking coffee while waiting for Chuck to arrive and begin his study. He turned to David, grabbed his arm, and said quietly, "I want you to know how blessed I am to know a man of conviction like your dad." He paused and David acknowledged his statement with a smile. "Now, I gotta go to work."

Pastor Chuck turned to walk toward the front of the room, but only got one step before he turned back to David. "By the way, the company your dad used to work for didn't just go out of business. The president embezzled over ten million dollars and fled the country. The other guys who masterminded the whole thing and tried to pin it on your dad ended up in jail." David must have looked shocked. Chuck gave him a thumbs up and said, "Conviction! Means different things to different people." He turned and marched toward the small podium at the front of the room and announced, "OK, let's get this thing going." The gathered folks responded with light applause and those standing took the remaining seats.

David found his mom and dad on the opposite side of the room. He got a cup of coffee before joining them.

David didn't get much out of the Bible study. He sat there amazed, pensive, glancing occasionally at his dad, a man of conviction. This was a man whom he thought had already taught him everything he was ever going to teach him in life. Now he could clearly see that he had a lot more to learn from him and from the God he knew.

They went to the church service after the 45-minute Bible study. Chuck did indeed talk about convictions versus principles in his sermon. He closed his message by saying, "If there are changes to be made in our lives, Christ must do the changing. If we try to do the changing on our own, we will fail. But if we seek Christ through His Word, through prayer, and through fellowship with other believers, then He will show us the way. He will convict us. And His word confirms that '*if any man is in Christ, he is a new creation. The old has passed away and the new has come.*'" David's mouth dropped open when he heard Pastor Chuck speak the same words that had popped into David's head the night before as he was going to sleep.

He turned to his dad.

"What's wrong, Son?" Jack asked.

"I gotta talk with you after the service."

Sylvia offered to sit in the back seat on the way home from church. "You tall guys sit up front now. Go ahead."

David tried to measure his words regarding Jack's job situation. Sylvia asked, "Can you stay long enough to have a sandwich with us, David?"

"Sure, Mom. That'd be good." He turned to Jack. "I talked with Pastor Chuck . . . "

"He's a good man. I like him," Jack said.

" . . . about your job situation in Indiana."

Jack hesitated. "What did he tell you?"

"A lot more than you have."

"Look, David. It just happened. I had to deal with it. You were in college. It was too much to explain to you at the time. I'm sorry, but I didn't think you'd understand."

"I still don't."

"Well, my boss and another guy got mixed up in some illegal stuff—money laundering, kickbacks. I found out about it and threatened to blow the whistle. I didn't realize the big boss was in on it too. They suggested I take a leave of absence or, better yet, get a new job. They didn't want to out-and-out fire me because they knew that I knew most everything that was going on. So I took the job here in Chicago. I thought everything would blow over or fall from its own weight, but then I caught word that things were heating up at the Indiana plant, and my bosses were going to try and pin things on me, saying the reason I left was because I didn't want to get caught. They were trying to shift the blame to me and cover their tracks. I went to Pastor Chuck and he really helped me through it. We got a lawyer and hired a private investigator."

"The big boss skipped town with the money?"

"He skipped the country. My boss and his crony got sent to federal prison in Joliet."

Sylvia reached forward, putting her hand on David's shoulder. "Dad's even gone to visit them in jail."

Jack passed by his wife's comment about the jail. "I kept good notes. I had some solid witnesses. And the truth came out.

"Wait a minute!" said David. "You've visited them in prison?"

"Yes, a couple of times. They made some mistakes, David. Some big mistakes. But I thought, you know, those guys were my friends, my coworkers for several years. They got caught up in something and they went over the edge. It happens. They needed to know that some mistakes are bad, but they're not fatal. A guy can lose all hope in prison unless he has something solid to hold on to."

David slumped back into his seat in stunned silence. Sylvia patted him on the shoulder and sat back in her seat, too, as they turned the corner toward home. They pulled into the driveway and stopped close to the garage. Jack left the car outside. He turned off the engine and looked at David. "You OK?" he asked.

"Yeah. It's a lot to digest all at once."

Sylvia chimed in, "Well, come inside and we'll digest something better."

Over lunch, the three of them talked more about Jack's previous job situation. Jack explained more of the details, while David had more questions. It intrigued him so much because it was a part of his dad's life he had not known existed. As they talked, a spiritual strength was revealed that David had not recognized was such a strong part of his dad's character. They talked about praying for guidance and strength; about praying for the men who were trying to frame him; and then later about praying with them in prison. David was clearly perplexed at the serious circumstances and his obliviousness at the time it happened, but at the same time he was impressed with his dad's inner strength. He was certainly a man of conviction.

David packed his bag for the trip home. Sylvia filled David's ice cooler with three cans of pop and ice from their freezer. They said their good-byes and I Love Yous. David knew he would still have to sort through all of the new information he'd received, but he also knew that he had six hours to devote to going over it.

Jack and Sylvia watched as David backed out of the driveway. He shifted the Caprice into drive and looked toward his parents, standing in the driveway near the house. They waved, as did David. Then David drove down the street. Sylvia continued to wave as he drove out of sight. She turned to her husband.

"He looked a little confused," she said.

"Yeah," he replied. "I think his eyes got opened a little this weekend."

"Jack, maybe we should have told David more about your job situation when it was happening."

"No. He wouldn't have been able to handle it at the time. He was in college. He was playing baseball and in love with that what's-her-name girl from Indiana."

"Cheryl, Jack. Her name was Cheryl."

"Whatever, Momma. The point is that the job situation was handled. It's over, and David's going to have to live with it."

Sylvia glanced down the street again, toward the corner where David's car had turned out of sight. "He just looked so confused, Jack."

Jack moved closer to his wife and put his arm around her. "It's called growing up. That's a good thing. He'll work it out. He's turning into a fine young man. You saw to that."

She smiled at Jack as she slipped her arm around his waist. "But he's my baby."

"I thought I was your baby." They both smiled warmly at each other. She nuzzled her head into Jack's shoulder as they walked with their arms around each other toward their home, which safely harbored the kitchen table, the pictures on the wall, the books, and their ever-growing love.

* * * * *

It was nearly dark. Snake's flunky pointed the headlights at the abandoned gas station.

"Wait here. And keep the lights on. I gotta check something," Snake said. He grabbed a flashlight and slithered out of the car to check the place out, poking the light beam through the dirty glass garage door window to get a better view. He prowled around to the back of the building—where he spotted the black Camaro.

"Makes sense," he muttered. "Now I know where she's at."

THIRTEEN

Money laundering. Kickbacks. Prison. Those were terms David didn't use in casual conversation. Sure, he knew about them, being in the business world and not totally naive. However, when he heard those phrases in conjunction with his easygoing, soft-spoken, well-read father, he got a little spooked.

And what was all this reliance on prayer? Jack had always been a churchgoer. Sylvia organized the family for the weekly visit to church service, but Jack gave David the real incentive to go: "Church first. Baseball after. No church? No baseball." That was all the motivation David needed.

David knew about God. He knew about Jesus. He knew He died on the cross for him. However, it was only one of the many facets of his life, particularly during his childhood. There were other aspects that were higher on the priority ladder than God. Baseball. Girls. College. Career. Everything else was virtually on the same level as God. His new home. Friends. Music. Fashion. The weather. His relationship with his parents was lumped into that lesser category.

The six-hour drive went by quickly because of the heavy subject matter David was thinking about. He knew the road well, so the trip went smoothly, and he talked out loud to himself along the way, processing all the new information he'd received.

Why can't I talk out loud to God? If He really does love me and cares about my life, maybe talking with him on a more personal level isn't such a bad idea.

"OK, Lord," David said out loud, glancing up to the sky, "It's me, David Freeman. I feel like I'm introducing myself to You again. Would You mind if I called on You a little more? I don't want to bug You a lot, but if this turbo-praying thing that my dad is into works for him, then I don't see why it wouldn't work for me. I really need some help sorting through my dad's situation. And I could always use some help with my job. The Cubs are gonna need some help this year, especially when they play the Cardinals. And then there's this girl, Joani Givens. I suppose you already know her." David wondered whether she had ever called out to God.

"God, I thank you for my parents and my home and my job—I already mentioned my job, didn't I?—and this car and my health and this nice day . . . " *Wow, that's already a lot of stuff I've never really considered being thankful for,* David thought.

"And I thank you for music and baseball and . . . " He looked around the inside of his car. " . . . and this can of pop and that bag of cookies my mom gave me." David was silent for another moment. "And my mom and dad's church, for Pastor Chuck, and for my church and Pastor Brunette." He looked toward the west. "And that's really a nice sunset, too. I really do have a lot to be thankful for."

The hours flew by and David found himself close to home. He closed off his "praying out loud" session and concentrated on making the final turns for home. He hit the garage door opener and pulled the Caprice into his neatly arranged, clean garage. "Look at all this stuff I've got: lawnmower, lawn tools, ball gloves, bats and balls, even that garbage can to put my garbage in. I guess I never knew what all I had."

This praying and thanking God thing is all right. I'm going to continue this. "Thanks, God," he said out loud. "I ought to make it a habit to pray at least twice a day—once in the morning and once at night." He started mentally adding a slot to his day-timer. "I'll call it: Talk to God Time. How long? Five minutes? No, make it at least ten. This is going to work out well."

David felt euphoric. "What a refreshing weekend I've had. Thanks, God."

He sorted out his clothes and put the dirty ones in the laundry basket and the clean ones in the dresser. He got out the Bill McCartney book and put in on the nightstand next to his bed. *Maybe I'll read some of that tonight. Yep, I feel pretty good.*

* * * * *

Joani sat on the front porch of her aunt and uncle's farmhouse near Fair Grove. She dangled her feet over the dry dirt of the meager flower bed that she stared at, and she scraped the toes of her shoes occasionally on the firm Missouri soil. She raised her head and watched the sun set completely behind the distant field, between two old trees that graced the front yard. A cool night breeze blew through. It felt good against her face, but made goose bumps raise on her bare arms.

She had gotten very drunk at a little tavern in Fair Grove on Friday night, slept in the next morning, ate very little all day Saturday, and was still feeling the effects of her Friday night escapade at dusk on Sunday. June and Herb had kept their distance most of the weekend. June asked her once if she wanted anything to eat that Sunday afternoon. Joani obliged and had some homemade bread and a slice of cheese with a glass of tea. It helped make her headache go away, but now, five hours later, it was starting to return. The vision of her escaping far away, to the west coast, was fading from her mind like the sun that was setting on the horizon before her.

Instead, Joani imagined her mom driving up the farm driveway. How great would that be, to see her, a healthy, smiling, vibrant woman, getting out of her car and jogging up to the front porch to give Joani a warm hug. She could tell Joani how much she'd missed her and that she had come to take her home. Not to the ramshackle apartment in St. Louis, but to a real home of their own. Maybe in Springfield, or up the road in Bolivar. Yeah, Bolivar. Mom was finishing up her degree at Southwest Baptist University, and soon Joani would be enrolling in classes at the University of Missouri in Columbia. She'd go to basketball games and dances and take classes and graduate and make something of her life.

The screen door screeched as Aunt June slowly approached Joani on the front porch. "Sun's gone down," she said as she advanced, cautiously.

Joani had been known to fly off the handle for no particular reason, but she responded to June's sunset comment with a muffled "yeah."

Joani sniffed once, obviously crying softly. June stood beside her and touched Joani's long hair at the back of her head. When Joani looked up, June saw the tears rolling down her cheeks. She pulled up a chair to sit close to her. Joani rested her head and arm on June's knee.

"What's wrong?" June said tenderly.

"I miss my mom," Joani said.

"I do too, honey. I do too."

FOURTEEN

It was a beautiful Sunday morning. David parked his car toward the rear of the church parking lot and enjoyed the walk to the sanctuary. Paul Brunette, an acquaintance from the church softball team was parking his minivan in the same row. He was also in sales and a good athlete like David. His brother John was the pastor of Faith Lutheran.

"Hi, David," said Paul. "How's it going?"

"Good. Great day, eh?"

"We should be out playing softball," said Paul. "Hey, what do you have going after church today?" he added, changing the subject abruptly.

David thought for a moment as they continued to walk. "Nothing, I guess."

"Angela and I have wanted to have you over for dinner. How about today after the service?"

"Yeah, sure," said David. "What's cookin'?"

"We always have a big meal after church on Sunday. And we like to invite different people from the church to join us. We haven't had much of a chance to talk outside of softball. And Angela's a great cook. You can just follow us home after church."

"OK." David didn't know Paul well, but he seemed like a nice guy, maybe even a "hoss." *I might be able to pick up some sales pointers from him this afternoon.*

The sermon that morning was about setting your life clock to God's timing. *Some good thoughts* David noted.

Paul and Angela's van turned into their driveway while David parked in the street. The kids jumped out immediately after the van stopped. Angela reminded them to change their clothes before playing outside. "And you can't play too long," she said. "We'll be having lunch soon." As David walked up the driveway, Angela smiled and said, "Hi, David. I'm Angela, Paul's wife. We're really glad you could join us."

"Thanks. It's not often I get a home-cooked meal, being a single guy."

"Come on in and relax. Dinner will be ready soon."

Paul welcomed David into his home and ushered him back to a spacious family room.

"This is a great room," David said.

"We practically live in this room," Paul said.

"How long have you been in this house?" David asked.

"Almost ten years. With all these kids running through, it's hard to figure how it's still standing. Can I get you something to drink, David?"

"Water's fine."

"You're not hard to please," Paul said. "One water, coming up."

Angela scurried about the kitchen, putting vegetables on the stove and getting a large salad bowl out of the refrigerator.

"What's for lunch?" David asked her.

"Oh, I put a roast in the oven this morning before church and it kind of cooks itself. And we've got veggies and mashed potatoes and salad."

"You making biscuits, hon?" Paul asked.

"Yeah, can't forget the biscuits," she replied. "And strawberry pie, too."

"We're in for a treat," Paul said with wide eyes. "My brother John's coming over, too, with his kids. His wife Julie isn't feeling well, so she went home after church to get some rest. And we also invited the Wilsons. You know them?"

"No, I don't think so. You've got a houseful coming over."

"We usually do, every Sunday. It's our way of getting to know more people from church."

"What's it like having a brother as a pastor?" David asked.

"Actually I've got three brothers who are pastors. And my dad is a pastor, too."

"How'd you end up in sales?"

"Somebody had to make some money," he laughed. "Actually, I didn't get the call like they all did."

The front door opened and Pastor John and his children came in without knocking. "Anybody home?" he called out.

"Back here, John," said Paul.

John ushered an older couple in their sixties down the hall toward the family room. He spied David standing off to the side and stuck out his hand to shake. "Hi, David. Good to see you. Do you know the Wilsons?"

David shook hands with Mr. Wilson and nodded at Mrs. Wilson, who didn't offer her hand. "Hi, I'm David Freeman. Nice to meet you."

"Thank you. Same here," said Mr. Wilson who, along with his wife, looked a little unsure about the casual atmosphere surrounding dinner with their pastor. They were both dressed in formal Sunday clothes. Mrs. Wilson held on to the strap of her small black purse with both hands. Paul offered to take Mr. Wilson's suit coat jacket, but he said he was OK, so Paul didn't press the issue.

Pastor John drew up close to David and whispered, "Let's hope Paul eats too much so we can whup him later on the basketball court out back."

"That's the only way you're gonna whup me," Paul boasted. The two of them grabbed each other and playfully pushed each other around. Mr. and Mrs. Wilson sat on the couch and stoically observed everything.

Angela called out from the kitchen. "Dinner's ready, everyone." Six adults and seven children gathered in the kitchen. "Let's pray," said Paul. He reached out and grabbed David's hand on one side and Angela's on the other. Everyone holding hands for prayer came quite naturally to both Brunette families, even the children, but it caught the Wilsons by surprise. Mrs. Wilson fumbled with the purse she was still holding, but managed to hang it over her elbow. Ten-year-old Christina, one of Paul's kids, reached up and grabbed her hand, and Mrs. Wilson smiled for the first time since she had arrived.

"Dear Lord," Paul said as everyone bowed. "We thank you for this food we're about to receive, the hands that prepared this food, and the friends we will enjoy this time with. We pray that Julie can get some good rest this afternoon and feel better. And we thank you for two full years this month of good health for Christina." He raised his eyes and smiled at Christina who smiled back but was embarrassed by the attention. "Thank you for Your love for us and the opportunities to love others. We pray this in Jesus' name. Amen." Everyone answered with an "Amen," even the Wilsons, although it was a beat after everyone else. It was a hint that they were starting to relax.

The plan was for the adults to eat the home cooked meal off the Brunettes' best china in the formal dining room while the children gathered around the kitchen table.

Mrs. Wilson spoke for the first time since she'd arrived. "Everything looks just lovely, Angela. You are a wonderful hostess." Mr. Wilson took his jacket off and hung it on the back of his chair. When he unbuttoned the cuffs of his long-sleeved white shirt and started rolling them up, Mrs. Wilson gave him a surprised look, as though he had made an inexcusable social faux pas. He smiled and rolled up the second sleeve to give her the unmistakable signal that he was feeling comfortable being there—and that he was ready to do some serious eating.

The food tasted incredible, and the conversation was light and simple. Mr. Wilson mentioned to Pastor John that he had thought about the possibility of being a pastor when he was a young man. Mrs. Wilson shot him a quizzical look, like she had never heard that before. David noticed it and wondered if he would be getting an earful later at home.

"Paul, I was curious about your prayer of thanks for two years of good health for Christina," David inquired. "She looks pretty healthy today."

"That hasn't always been the case," Paul said. "She was diagnosed with Ewing's sarcoma when she was six. It's a rare cancer on the spine. The doctors told us she had less than a fifty percent chance of survival."

"How awful that must have been for all of you," Mrs. Wilson remarked, sounding quite grandmotherly.

Angela replied, "It was a whole year of intense treatment and intense prayer. But I think the experience strengthened the faith of each of us."

Paul put down his fork, put his elbows on the table, and clasped his hands in front of his face to concentrate on telling the details of Christina's treatment. "We had relatives and friends from all over the country praying for Christina. The radiation and chemotherapy treatments were tough enough for a grown-up to handle, let alone a six-year-old child. We spent a lot of hours at the oncology clinic at Cardinal Glennon

Children's Hospital in St. Louis."

"At one point," Angela said, "Christina couldn't eat, drink, or even swallow. For two months!"

Pastor John added, "And her temperature rose so high, they didn't think she was going to make it."

"There were several times when the doctors told us to prepare for the worst," Paul said.

Angela smiled warmly and said, "But each time, we prayed, and our friends and family prayed, and God took care of each crisis. And today, she's cancer free."

Mrs. Wilson remarked, "That must have been so hard on all of you."

"Christina was a warrior," Paul said. "A year later, the cancer reappeared in the exact same spot." Mrs. Wilson gasped. "The doctor said that was common for this type of cancer. Again, they told us to expect the worst. And again we surrounded the situation with prayer. And the next week the X-rays showed that there was only scar tissue where the cancer had been." Everyone at the table exhaled with relief.

"They had no explanation," Pastor John added.

Mr. Wilson chimed in: "Folks don't think miracles happen these days, but I disagree. We just don't recognize them, or we just don't think to ask God to intercede in a difficult situation." Mrs. Wilson looked admiringly at her husband for his statement of faith, as if she were thinking he might actually have made a good pastor.

"Who wants strawberry pie?" Angela asked, temporarily breaking the conversational heaviness.

After the pie and more conversation, the Wilsons excused themselves for having to rush off right away. "We hate to eat and run, you know," Mrs. Wilson said, "but we're supposed to meet our daughter and her husband and children later this evening. I hope you'll forgive us. We've really had a wonderful time." Paul walked the Wilsons to the front door while Pastor

John and David retreated to the living room.

"Take that big chair, David. It's the best chair," Pastor John said.

"Isn't that Paul's chair?" David asked.

"Sure. That's why you need to get it before he gets back in here."

Paul had asked Angela if she needed some help with the dishes. "No!" she responded quickly. "You guys would be in the way." Paul kissed her on the cheek and joined David and John in the family room.

David patted the arms of the overstuffed chair. "Nice chair, Paul."

"Be careful. You might fall asleep in that chair. It's happened before," he responded.

John flipped channels on the television to see if there was a ballgame on. The boy caught the last three innings of the Cardinals game as St. Louis took the L.A. Dodgers to the cleaners. The conversation was mostly about baseball. When the ballgame ended, John turned off the TV just as an obnoxious commercial for an upcoming sitcom started to air. Angela had finished her work and disappeared to another part of the house while the children were playing in the backyard.

"You eat too much?" John said as he looked toward Paul.

"Yeah, and now I'm probably about as slow as you," he answered.

"Those are fightin' words," John said as they both doubled up their fists, but then leaned back into the couch, laughing.

"You guys always this competitive?" David remarked. "What's it like when all *four* brothers get together?"

"You don't want to know," Paul said.

"It can get pretty bloody," John admitted.

"Good thing your dad was a pastor," said David. "I'll bet he was a good referee."

"He was always separating us," Paul said. "I'm sure he did a lot of praying that we wouldn't kill each other before we grew up and moved out."

"And now three of you are pastors?" David added.

"Somebody has to make some money," John said as he looked at Paul, winking.

Paul looked at David and said, "See, I told you that was the reason."

"Actually, we all get along pretty well," John said. "We're just competitive by nature."

"No, we're not," said Paul.

"Yes, we are," John answered.

"No, we're not."

"Yes, we are."

"You ready to go one-on-one?"

"No," sighed John. "I'm beat. I should get home and see how Julie's doing."

"She's probably enjoying the quiet. Just sit down for a while."

They talked about sports and family and work, but Jesus was also interwoven into the conversation. David could tell from their ease at bringing up their faith that these two were men of conviction, just like Pastor Mueller had talked about. David mentioned the sermon he had heard a couple of weeks earlier in Roselle and how Pastor Chuck had brought out the differences between a man of principle and a man of conviction. John and Paul both knew Chuck quite well. "That sounds like something he would say," Paul said.

"Probably took the idea from his dad," John added.

"Oh, like you've never done that?" Paul added. The brothers were at it again, but they ceased their playful jabbing when Angela entered the room.

"You guys OK? You want anything?" she asked.

"No, hon," Paul answered. "We're OK. Great dinner." John and David agreed.

"Just doin' my part for the Kingdom," she quipped.

John turned his attention back to David. "So, David, how long you been going to church?"

"All my life. But I gotta admit that lately I've been getting into it a little deeper."

"How so?" John asked.

"Well, my dad went through a big job change several years ago when I was in college. And I found out that there was more to it than just changing jobs. Seems he caught his bosses doing some illegal stuff, and they tried to pin it all on him. He handled it OK, but it kind of threw me for a loop."

"You just thought he was changing jobs?" Paul asked.

"Yeah. And I also found out that he spent a lot of time praying about the situation."

"Well, he was pointed in the right direction," John said.

"Yeah, but he'd never been a real religious guy before, not openly. He went to church, and he'd always been a straight-up guy. But he said some stuff like he 'gave the situation over to the Lord,' and he spent a lot of time in prayer with Pastor Mueller. It just didn't sound like him—or at least the guy I thought he was."

"Like I said, he was pointed in the right direction," John said.

"This whole thing has gotten me to start praying more and being thankful for all the things that I have," said David, "but I just . . . " he hesitated.

"Just what?" Paul asked.

"Am I missing something? Is there something else out there? I mean, something bigger? Something more to this church thing, this Christian thing?"

"Yes," said John. "There's *always* something more. Jesus is always leading and guiding us, giving us opportunity to grow in faith and learn more about Him."

"Well, I started praying more, but it feels like I'm missing something."

"You just need to hang in there and continue getting to know God," said Paul. "Talking about it like this with other Christian guys is a good way to work things out."

John took a pastoral tone. "Your dad went through a really traumatic experience, and it sounds like he really grew spiritually from it. We all did when Christina went through her cancer treatments. It sounds like you're also benefiting from your dad's situation by taking a good look at your own spiritual walk. You hang in there. God's going to show *you* the way, too."

"You know what you need to do?" Paul said. "You need to come with us to Promise Keepers in Indianapolis." David's mouth dropped open. "A bunch of us from church are going up there in a couple of weeks. I think we've got some extra tickets."

John joined in Paul's enthusiasm. "Yeah, that's a great idea. You'll love it, David. A whole bunch of guys singing and sharing . . . "

"I know," David admitted, raising his hand in a stop signal. "My dad mentioned that some guys from his church were going, and he suggested I go with them."

"There's your confirmation, if you need it," said John.

"OK, it sounds good. I'll do it."

"Great," Paul said. "Now, how about some more strawberry pie?"

* * * * *

David called his mom and dad that night and told them about the lunch at Paul's and how he was planning to go to the Promise Keepers rally in Indianapolis with the group from his church. They were both pleased, and Jack said he'd try to meet up with him there. "Although it might be kind of tough," he added. "They're planning on seventy thousand guys being there."

"Seventy thousand?" David was shocked. "I didn't realize it was going to be *that* big."

"That's quite a *koinonia* group, isn't it?" his dad remarked.

"A what?"

"*Koinonia*. It's a Greek word for a special bond, a close-knit fellowship group."

"You're learning Greek now?" David asked, a smile in his voice.

"Just something I picked up," his dad said.

"Have you been able to talk with that girl you mentioned?" his mom asked.

With all of the changes in David's life, he really hadn't thought about Joani lately. "No, Mom. I really haven't."

"Well, I was just asking," she said.

"OK. I gotta go. Got a big day at work tomorrow."

* * * * *

"Uncle Herb, would you run me out to Jackson's Station tomorrow so I can pick up my car?" Joani asked.

"Your car?" Herb asked, looking up from reading his newspaper.

"Yeah, I think it's time I start thinkin' about movin' on and makin' something of my life."

June overheard the conversation while washing dishes in the kitchen sink. She prayed: *Lord, she needs more than a car to help her get her life straightened out. She needs You. Help her to find You.*

FIFTEEN

The group from Faith Lutheran in St. Louis drove up I-70 and straight into downtown Indianapolis where the Promise Keepers rally was being held at the stadium where the Indianapolis Colts play football. The church had taken two vanloads of men for the day-and-a-half conference, and as they weaved into the parking lot with the steady stream of vehicles, they could see cars, vans, and buses everywhere.

From the moment he arrived, David was astounded by the event's atmosphere. There were thousands of guys—all shapes and sizes and colors of guys—gathering on a Friday night for the opening session and then again all day Saturday. *We get a lunch meal on Saturday with this?* David said. *How they gonna feed all these guys?*

As the men exited their vans, they grabbed their Bibles and notebooks and headed toward the stadium. Several of the guys had been to PK rallies before and had told the others what they could expect. Most of the group was new at this and appreciated the words.

David had entertained thoughts that he would run into his dad and the group from his church in the parking lot or at least walking toward the stadium. Or maybe Jack would be standing around outside the entrance waiting for him. However, as they approached the massive stadium, it was obvious that David's vision of the scope of this event had been too small. The sheer number of men gathering was staggering.

Around the outside of the stadium, the walkways were filled with two lines of men, six to ten wide, going in opposite directions. One group was moving toward one entrance and the other group was winding toward an entrance on the opposite end of the stadium. There was lots of energetic talking and slow shuffling. Occasionally, a man would recognize someone he knew who was pushing in the opposite direction and shout out to him over the top of the mass in motion.

As they came upon several sets of doors, all eighteen men from Faith Lutheran filed into the Dome. They had managed to stay together among the throng, even though they didn't have matching T-shirts like several groups were wearing—same-color shirts with the same message on the front or back, things like:

Offshore Christian Men's Fellowship

Orland Park Baptist Church

New Vision Fellowship

Another group all wore fluorescent yellow hats that read First Assembly.

Pastor John led the group from Faith as they walked down

about fifty steps to the stadium floor. David gazed at the sea of male humanity that was eagerly filling up the arena seats. Pastor John carved out a path toward the center of the floor seats.

The men staked off six seats in each of three rows off one of the middle aisles, about forty rows back from the huge stage. Recorded music was coming from the two banks of speakers hoisted high above each side of the stage. David couldn't make out any words the singer was singing, but the rhythmic beat of the bass and the drums was infectious. *Incredible! Dad told me there wouldn't be anything like this, and he was right.*

Guys. Young and old. Most looked like they were part of a group, but there were also a few sitting by themselves. Most were dressed casually in slacks and T-shirts. Occasionally, David saw someone in a sport coat and tie, but it was rare. He stood there looking up and out and around, drinking in the atmosphere and reading various T-shirt slogans: *Adidas, Huntsville Fire Fighters, Stan Burgess Windshield Repair,* and so forth.

He couldn't help but notice the contrast in a couple of the messages. One read: Cancun. A guy near him had a shirt that read: Reflect the Son.

A teenager had a T-shirt that boasted "If you were hot, I'd be dating you," while an older gentleman in the same group had one that read "Real Men Follow Jesus."

There were lots of hats, too.

Chicago Bears

Promise Keepers

Hope Seeds

There were boys with their fathers. Timid guys. Bold guys.

Friendly guys. Black guys and white guys shaking hands, hugging, laughing. Some ethnic groups were mixing and some were huddled in their tribes.

How many of these guys are accountants? How many are factory workers? Who are the salesmen? The pastors? The group from David's church fit in very well. They were diverse in appearance, pretty much like the entire stadium. They were simply an extension of the group from Faith Lutheran, multiplied by two thousand, and growing!

David thought: *This is the kind of crowd you'd go to a football game with. Not an NFL game, though, a* high school *game. This is a mixed bag and an informal group. These are men you would feel comfortable having over to your home for a cookout.* The overhead screens flashed messages.

Deaf section on the floor at the foot of the stage.

First Aid on the first floor east concourse.

Radios en espanol en la parte de atras de el piso principal.

The music kept playing in the background, helping to guide the character of the surroundings. Some men in his group were sitting down. Some men were standing up and talking, taking in the scenery. Paul Brunette slapped David on the shoulder. "Pretty cool, eh?" he said.

"Yeah. I had no idea. This is great," David responded.

A group from one of the middle sections on the side of the arena shouted out, slowly but also in unison,

"We ... love ... Jesus. Yes ... we ... do
We ... love ... Jesus. How... 'bout ... *you*?"

Then, they cheered. Another group on the opposite side of

the arena chanted the same sentences a little louder.

"We ... love ... Jesus. Yes ... we ... do
We ... love ... Jesus. How... 'bout ... *you*?"

They cheered a little louder also, and that egged on the group on the other side of the arena to begin organizing more men to form a bigger group to answer back.

"We ... love ... Jesus. Yes ... we ... do
We ... love ... Jesus. How... 'bout ... YOU?"

David wanted his section to start cheering. But then his whole focus changed as a beach ball bounced off his shoulder. Someone else tipped it up in the air as it caromed off him, and then another guy bashed the ball fifteen yards away. The crowd around David shouted and laughed and ardently followed the ball as it was tipped and batted across the lower arena. Some men were eagerly following the ball, and some were as surprised as David had been when it invaded their line of sight. There was anticipation, then disappointment, as the ball went in the opposite direction . . . then anticipation again. The entire right side of the upper arena now called out in unison.

"We ... love ... Jesus. Yes ... we ... do
We ... love ... Jesus. How... 'bout ... YOU?"

They pointed to the left side of the stadium and cheered loudly, encouraging that side to outdo their effort. David saw three more beach balls appear across the horizon, then two more behind him. The crowd had swelled to three-quarters capacity; there were probably fifty thousand men in the stadium by now.

The atmosphere was electric. The overhead screen signs read:

The Challenge

A group of six guys, three black and three white, formed a huddle in the aisle and was praying together. Guys kept filing into the arena. The floor was filled by now. Only the upper sections of the arena were available. "There must be sixty thousand in here," David shouted to Paul Brunette, standing next to him.

"I think you're right. And they're still coming in," Paul said.

> "We ... love ... Jesus. Yes ... we ... do
> We ... love ... Jesus. How... 'bout ... *YOU?*"

David shouted out the last line with the others. Some of the guys on the floor tried to organize the section around the group from Faith Lutheran to answer the upper arena's cheers. The screen sign now read:

> *There is a prayer booth*
> *at the southeast corner*
> *in the back of the arena.*

David thought: *I should visit the prayer booth just to thank God for the opportunity to be here.* A tech guy was on stage. He had headphones and was talking with someone on his remote microphone. The music continued over the speakers. The left side of the arena erupted:

> "We ... love ... Jesus. Yes ... we ... do
> We ... love ... Jesus. How... 'bout ... *YOU?*"

Then the loudest cheer of the night. The leaders of the floor people were still getting organized. David thought they almost had it. Three men stood up on their chairs and counted off "one . . . two . . . three."

> "We ... love ... Jesus. Yes ... we ... do
> We ... love ... Jesus. How... 'bout ... *YOU*?"

It wasn't as loud as the upper sections, but it was only this group's first attempt. It was a good start. And now David noticed still more t-shirts: *Indianapolis Colts, Michigan Wolverines, Real Men Seek Jesus.*

Where's my dad? David thought. *I hope he's here and drinking all of this in, too. My dad? Wait a minute. My dad suggested I come to something like this?* David remembered that his dad was the man who prayed and worked through a horrendous job situation and came out the other side as a man of conviction. *Is this where he got that conviction? That's not too hard of a possibility to grasp. And I guess that if this atmosphere could touch him, it could touch anyone, including me. I hope I can talk with him sometime while I'm here and tell him how grateful I am that he suggested I come to this.*

The band members walked on stage, taking up their instruments. Bass, drums, guitar, keyboard. Some guys in the arena were sitting through this. David saw a couple of men by themselves reading their program guide. *What's wrong with them? Don't they want to be a part of the electricity that's flowing through this place?*

The arena was almost full now. There were only a few empty seats toward the top. Many seats behind the stage also were filled. They couldn't possibly see the screens, but they were the only seats available in the arena.

Welcome to Promise Keepers – Indianapolis!

The tech guy with the headphones left the stage. A singer stepped to the microphone. "Gentlemen!" his voice boomed out over the stadium, echoing off the back walls. "Gentlemen, welcome to Promise Keepers, Indianapolis, Indiana!" Cheers. Loud cheers. Whistles. Clapping. Hands raised in the air. Shouting.

The main board read, quite simply:

The Challenge.

SIXTEEN

The band started playing. The crack of the drums. The solid boom of the bass. The keyboard. The guitar. The singer confidently encouraged the crowd, "Keep clapping your hands for God, men." Everyone was clapping on the beats of two and four. That was not an easy thing to do for the rhythmically challenged like David. However, he saw that there were guys around him who also wanted to clap on beats one and three, but were quickly converted to two and four. Seventy thousand men clapping on two and four! The singer began, and the words appeared on the bottom of the screen, below the video picture of the singer. Everyone was singing along. David remembered this song from Pastor Chuck's church. He thought they might have sung it at his church, too. *Maybe I wasn't listening. It certainly wasn't this loud, this big.*

Men were raising their hands. David wanted to, but he'd

never done that before. *Why are they raising their hands? It looks natural for most of them. It feels contrived for me.* David kept on clapping his hands. Two and four. He heard himself sing out.

The singers sang the chorus over and over, and David didn't want the song to end. It felt fresh each time they sang it.

He raised his right hand while he sang. He wasn't sure why he did it, but now it felt more natural. The songleader motioned for the band to cut out and stuck the microphone out toward the crowd as he encouraged them to "take it." David brought his hand down and started clapping again. *I hope they'll sing this again at my church sometime soon. I'll recognize it for sure this time. I'll sing along. I may even clap on two and four!*

The song ended. The crowd cheered. The lights went down. A video of a race car started playing on the screens. The audio was realistic. It sounded like an actual Indy car was racing through the arena. A spotlight shown down on the aisle behind David. An older black man was driving a golf cart decked out to resemble a '57 Chevy. He had a microphone attached to the steering wheel and was slapping hands with men as he drove slowly down the aisle. "Hey, guys. How you doin'? Hey, Indianapolis. Hey, guys." The car noise kept blaring over the speakers as the man drove his way toward the front of the stage. A video camera projected his progress across the large screens. "Hey, guys. Hey, Indianapolis. You glad you're here?" The crowd clapped and cheered as he made his way to the stage.

He parked the cart at the front of the stage and grabbed the microphone. He faced the crowd as the applause died down and he shouted, "Welcome to Promise Keepers, Indianapolis! We're glad you're here!" The crowd cheered. The man walked up a ramp that looked like a bridge leading up to the stage. "We are so glad you're here." He turned to face the crowd and continued his walk toward the podium at the front center portion of the stage. "My name is Raleigh Washington. I'm from Chicago, and I'll be your emcee for the weekend." Another cheer went up. David had no idea who Raleigh Washington was, but he cheered anyway. "During the next twenty-four hours, I hope we're going to get to know each other really well." The cheering died down and everyone took their seats.

Raleigh waited as the chairs shuffled and movement came to a stop. "You know, when I was a young man, we used to look at each other . . . you know, the brothers . . . " The crowd laughed and cheered. "The brothers used to look at each other and say, 'Yo, blood.' We may not have known the guy, but we would say, 'Yo, blood.' Well, men, all of us here in this arena are connected by the blood of Jesus." Another cheer went up. "And so, this weekend we're all gonna greet each other with 'Yo, blood.' So: Yo, blood!"

The crowd shouted, "Yo, blood!"

Raleigh countered, "Yo, blood!"

The crowd shouted louder, "Yo, blood!"

"That's right," Raleigh said. "God is going to visit us here this weekend." The crowd enthusiastically shouted its approval. "Men, let's get this started right with a word of prayer. Will you pray with me?" Men immediately stood, removed their hats, and bowed their heads.

> *"Lord, we are glad You have brought us to this place.*
> *We pray for everyone gathered here that they may . . ."*

David half followed Raleigh's prayer and also prayed his own prayer. *Lord, what a great time already,* David prayed. *Everyone said this would be a great experience. It already has been. Lord, help me to hear everything I'm supposed to hear. And help me get some handles to hold on to in my life, my work, my church, maybe even my love life. Help me to know what are the right things to do in my life.* In the meantime, Raleigh was finishing his prayer . . .

> *" . . . Lord, we put this weekend into Your hands.*
> *We give it to You. All these things*
> *we pray in your name. Amen."*

It seemed like an entire stadium answered, "Amen." Hats went back on and a cheer went up from the crowd as many of the men, including David, took their seats. *They even cheered for the prayer,* David thought. *This was a fired-up group.*

Raleigh pointed toward the band. "Let's hear from the Maranatha Praise Band." The band started immediately. The crowd rose to its feet again. David did, too, as if pulled by the excitement of the men immediately around him. This song was as infectious as the one before it. David found himself singing along right away and even raising a hand. The words flowed across the screen. The melody was easy to catch.

Yes, Lord. Let Your mercy flow, David thought. *I know a lot of people who need mercy. I guess I could use some myself.*

So many thoughts went through David's mind. "If anyone is in Christ, he is a new creation. The old has passed away. The new has come." *In Christ? I'm in Christ, aren't I?*

God has really blessed me. His face has shined on me. David started counting his blessings again, just as he had been doing in his prayers since he came home from his parents' house that weekend. *My family, my work, my health, my home. My church, my friends, music, baseball. The little things. The big things. The abstract things. The very-much-real things.*

The band broke into a new song. The guys around David sang it with enthusiasm. Several of the men were lifting their hands and bouncing on their toes to the rhythm of the music. Their eyes were closed and it looked as if they were straining with every fiber of their being to convey the offering of praise directly to God.

God, You are incredible. Look how He's blessed us. Look how He's blessed me. The junior high reading class that David tutored came to mind. He judged that he was blessed in so many more ways than those poor kids. The neighborhood that they grew up in. The broken families that they came from. *How had God blessed them?*

"Lord, maybe there's a way to take those kids out of that environment so they can make something of their lives," he prayed. *Surely, God could do that. Yes, He could do that.*

David reached up to the heavens and closed his eyes as the band closed off the song and the crowd cheered. *God, You are incredible*, he thought.

Raleigh Washington now walked back to the podium. "Yo, blood!" he shouted.

"Yo, blood!" the huge crowd shouted back.

"That's right. Men," Raleigh said, "this weekend is called The Challenge. It is a call to action for men who are serious about their faith." David wondered if he was serious about his faith. *I must be. I'm here, aren't I?*

"You see this bridge up here?" Raleigh pointed to the bridge that reached from the floor to the stage. "We're going to build that bridge as the weekend goes along. You see, no man is an island . . . " That picture rolled around in David's head. "No man can stand alone. So we need to build bridges to each other. We need to be connected to each other, because we want to win the world for Christ." The crowd cheered its approval. "Now, direct your attention to the overhead screens."

A video began. It spoke of two astronauts who were Promise Keepers. The dramatic portrayal of these two men was inspiring. Then it dawned on David: *These two gave their lives in the Columbia disaster!*

David didn't even have time to fully digest the message of the first video when it went into a second one, a narrative of a rodeo rider hitting the shoot on top of an angry three thousand-pound bull. The cowboy was a Promise Keeper, too. The video was rolling along, the stadium filled with the booming sounds of . . .

"... demands a cowboy with guts of steel,
an undaunted will, and a tenacious heart.
He must be predisposed to grab fear by the reigns
and literally bury his stainless steel spurs
into the hide of that ferocious beast
and take him to the pinnacle of his fury."

God, I'm a salesman. These scenes make my work look so tame and ordinary. There's no comparison. My job is boring compared to these guys. Then came a video of a Marine Corps pilot. David presumed he was a Promise Keeper, too.

"... highly sophisticated Harrier jets that fly
just under the speed of sound and in
seemingly miraculous ingenuity can land
on the head of a silver dollar."

That's some precision, David thought.

"... has put twelve hundred hours into his Harrier jet and has
trained a hundred and twenty marine pilots. Together they
have provided air protection for our troops all over the world
with surface-to-air missiles and anti-aircraft fire nipping at
their heels. These courageous American pilots live the challenge. They risk their lives daily to let freedom ring in our sweet
land of liberty and for the stars and stripes that fly proudly
over our heads."

God bless America! David cheered with the rest of the men

watching the video. The background music then took a dramatic turn.

"But of all the spaceships and the astronauts who fought to fly
them; of all the bucking bulls and the cowboys who fought to
ride them; of all the wars and the warriors who fought to win
them, the fighting arena called Golgotha and the men who
fought there was without a doubt the most grueling, the most
demanding, the most consequential battleground mankind has
ever known."

The hair went up on the back of David's neck. The video went to the most gruesomely realistic depiction of a crucifixion scene he had ever witnessed, so radically different from any piece of artwork he had ever gazed at, so thoroughly unfamiliar to what he had imagined in his mind from his youth.

"Three crosses. Three men. Three lives.
Three stories. Three fighters.
All fighting to the bitter end."

David could not turn his eyes away from the shocking dramatization of Christ's agony, Christ's pain. The images tore at his heart and his mind and reached to the depths of his soul.

"Fighting in the middle of this notorious hill was the
one called Jesus. The Messiah. The one who would
become like us to give it all to win the souls of men."

David was seeing a Jesus he had never seen before.

"His requisition was the most demanding.
His fearlessness the most undaunting.
His courage the most unrelenting.

And His cause the most compelling."

If a man is in Christ, he is a new creation. The verse rolled over and over in David's head.

"Fighting on His left was a criminal, a thief. A man of pride."

I'm not that man, am I? I'm not a criminal. I'm not a thief. David hung his head. *But am I a man of pride? Pride in my frivolous human principles to make me successful in life? But they're good principles, aren't they, Lord?*

> *"A man committed to fight to the death.*
> *To stand his ground.*
> *To never give in.*
> *To finish as he started."*

Oh, God. I'm not that man, am I? There's a difference between this kind of fight and being a man of determination, isn't there?

> *"Like many men today, he'll live and die alone*
> *with no need for anyone to give him a helping hand.*
> *He'll ignore his mistakes.*
> *He'll dance away from the sin of guilt.*
> *He'll fight until he dies to be his own man."*

No, Lord. No! I'm a man of principle. No, a man of conviction. Tears came to David's eyes. *Lord, I can be taught. I can learn. I can become a new man, in Christ.*

> *"Fighting on the cross on the right side of Jesus*
> *is a different sort of criminal.*
> *He was a thief with a personal battle*

to overcome a shameful past.
To overcome his failures."

Am I the man on the right side of Jesus? My past isn't shameful. I haven't failed so often or fallen so hard that I've needed to overcome that much. Not like other people I've known. Not like Joani, or that Snake guy. The tears welled up again. What is this personal battle that is tearing at me?

"Like many of us in this arena,
he had fought so long and lost so much.
Battle fatigued and filled with failure,
he's ready to throw in the towel.
But he would fight to overcome himself
and look to the one in the middle
who will win for him his final victory."

What is my fight? I know there is a battle within me. How can I know what that battle is? How will I know when victory has occurred?

"These three were the challengers.
The rocky hillside known as the Skull
and the three Roman crosses that stood there
were their challenge."

What is my battle? What is this fight within me? Where is my victory? How will I know it? Is this my challenge?

"All three men were fighters in every sense of the word.
They would give it their all.
They would fight their cause to their last breath."

The video ended. A man in a boxing outfit—trunks, shoes,

gloves, warm-up coat—jogged up the aisle toward the front. There was a light bag set up. He began a rhythmic pounding of the bag, slowly at first, then faster and more powerfully, exactly like David's soul had been stirring in this arena—slowly at first, then faster and more powerfully.

God, I have no concept of who You are. Oh, God. I have so much to learn. Teach me. This is not mere feelings or emotion. I am convinced that I am being challenged by the cross of Jesus Christ.

* * * * *

It was nearly dark. Snake and the flunky had driven down nearly every street in Fair Grove. It didn't take long. Fair Grove was a very small town. During one of their rare peaceful conversations, Joani had chattered away to Snake about Fair Grove and the farm and her spending time there when she was growing up. And she had mentioned the gas station where, a couple of weeks earlier, Snake had discovered the Camaro had been stashed away. She harangued about how the owner had worked on her car and that it could outrun Snake's T-bird on a short or long track—straight, curved, narrow, wide, paved, or dirt.

Now several weeks since her escape, Snake knew he was close to finding her. He wasn't sure what he was going to do to her once he got her back within arm's reach, but he figured he'd decide that when the time came.

"Snake, you sure that girl is around here somewhere?" the flunky asked.

"I found her car, didn't I?" he boasted.

They passed a gas station and a burger joint as they slowly negotiated the road. The north-south four-lane highway at the edge of town was up ahead, less than a quarter mile away. Snake glanced to his left and saw an auburn-haired woman exit the liquor store with a small brown paper bag and get in a green Chevy Tudor. He strained his neck to get a closer look as the flunky kept his eyes on the road ahead. "That's her," he barked, startling the flunky. "Pull in over here," he demanded, pointing to the large supermarket parking lot on the right. "Park over there so I can see across the road," he ordered.

It was at least a hundred yards across the road and the sun wasn't much help at illuminating the area anymore today, but Snake was sure he'd found Joani Givens. He stared across the road as the girl sat still in her car for a minute or two. Then she pulled the brown paper bag close to her lips and tilted her head back, taking a drink of the elixir in the bottle hidden in the bag. She wiped her lips with the back of her sleeve and stared ahead for another minute or two. Then she took another drink. Snake was getting impatient with the girl. If he approached her now, she might cause a scene, he thought. But if he waited until she drove away, he might be able to get her alone on one of the dark country roads. Plus, he had to make sure the girl was actually Joani.

Snake didn't want Joani back because he was in love with her or anything remotely positive. He simply knew he could dominate her more strongly than most of the women he'd met. And she did know some details about his operation. That fact had hammered away at his safety since that day in Lebanon and had put him constantly on edge. And she had a dependable car—the Camaro. That was her greatest asset. His T-bird was a piece of junk.

The girl took another drink and started her car. The flunky went to start his car also but Snake motioned for him not to. "Not yet," he whispered. "Let's make sure it's her." The green Chevy pulled out of the liquor store and Snake got a good look at the driver as she drove in front of them back down the road toward town. It was Joani for sure. "OK, let's follow her. Not too close. Let's see where she's going."

Joani drove back through Fair Grove and then out of town toward the farm. She tried to fight back the tears of her lost heart as she took another sip of the whiskey. It burned all the way down, but it soothed her mind for a fleeting moment. The stupor was engaging and made her forget her past mistakes and her present uncertainties. She didn't even notice the car following her several hundred yards behind.

"Not too close!" Snake reminded the flunky. "This ain't a chase." The flunky followed Snake's instructions well. As the lights of Fair Grove got farther behind them, the flunky let more distance get between his car and the Chevy. It wasn't hard to follow the lights of the car on the dark country road.

As Joani turned to the right down a dirt road, Snake and the flunky slowed to a crawl and watched as she turned up a driveway toward a farmhouse a quarter-mile down the road.

"Kill your lights," Snake ordered. Their eyes quickly adjusted to the clear night, illuminated by the nearly full moonlight. They drove slowly and undetected toward the driveway that led to Joani's hiding place.

The flunky pulled to a gentle stop at the end of the driveway, across the road from the mailbox. Snake reached into his overnight bag and pulled out a flashlight, flipping the switch to make sure it worked and then shutting the light off quickly. He also grabbed his .38 pistol, spinning the chamber and inspecting it to make sure it was loaded. "You wait here. I'll be back soon," he told the stunned flunky, who didn't think Snake should resort to using a gun to persuade Joani to come back to St. Louis with him. Or maybe Snake was simply going to kill her. That would make the flunky an accessory to murder. He was in over his head for sure.

Snake exited the car quickly so the interior overhead light wouldn't be noticed, and then he closed the door quietly so as not to make any noise that would pierce the silent darkness. He crept across the road and down the driveway toward the house as the flunky waited nervously.

Snake saw Joani get out of the Chevy she parked in the circle drive and watched as she walked toward the living room lights of the farmhouse. He waited until she slowly negotiated the steps up to the porch and staggered into the house through the front door. Snake then slithered past the one-car garage and shined his flashlight through the garage door window. Parked inside was Joani's black Camaro. "Good. Gonna get those wheels back, too." He patted the .38 in his belt and skulked toward the house.

SEVENTEEN

The boxer pounded the light bag with fierce passion. The rhythm from his smacking of the punching bag with his taped fists was only hindered by his intensity. He was not hitting the bag for show; he was hitting it to take out his frustration. His eyes were focused on the bag as he breathed deeply from the workout. He finished with a teeth-clenched final blow and turned to jog up the bridge to the stage area, where several large wooden logs were piled.

He placed a black cloth skullcap on his head and grabbed a large crossbeam and threw it across a longer pole that was the same width. They had been precut so they would fit into the shape of a cross. It was obvious he was constructing a cross like the one Jesus and the two thieves had been nailed to. He shouted out,

"I will never give in!

I will never, ever, ever relent.
I am and I will always be my own man.
My own man!
I didn't need my father's hand to hold.
And I need no man's hand to hold today."

He nailed the two beams together at the center with large
spikes and breathed deeply from the exertion.

"I can make it on my own.
On my own!
No one's going to take away my independence.
No one!
I'll fight you.
I'll fight the system.
I'll fight God.
I'll fight any man.
And I may lose,
but I have lost before
and I can take my licks.
As long as I can stand my ground
and not give in
and maintain control,
I will win.
I will win.
I will win!"

David saw his own self, his independence, his simplistic
view of success, of life, of God. He wanted to keep control of it
all. He thought he could win at life on his own with his principles. The boxer turned his eyes upward.

"Hey, up there!
If you're the King of the Jews,

> *why don't you come down here*
> *and save yourself."*

The boxer lifted the cross straight up in the air with the help of another man. It stood well over fifteen feet high. His breathing was labored. Sweat was pouring off his face. He threw down the black skullcap and stumbled toward a second cross on the right.

> *"The war that wages within my heart*
> *is far greater than the physical battle I fight*
> *as I gasp for my last breath."*

Jesus Himself had not been real to David before this day, this hour. Now, He was being revealed to him before his eyes. "Therefore, if anyone is in Christ, he is a new creation; the old has gone, the new has come!" The boxer now put a white skullcap on his head and then lifted a second crossbeam and dropped it into a second pre-cut slot.

> *"How can I even look to the one*
> *who calls himself the God of love,*
> *the God of peace,*
> *the God of my salvation?*
> *I've never known love.*
> *I've never known my father's blessing."*

He began pounding the two logs together.

> *"In my search for his love, and in my anger*
> *over the resentment that has been in my heart,*
> *I have been led into the darkest alleys and deepest of sins.*
> *When I have tried to do right, I have failed.*
> *I know now that nothing good dwells in me.*

The wishing is present within me, but the doing of good is not.
My spirit is willing, but my flesh is weak.
I have fought to do the right thing, and I have failed.
Now I fight to look to the only one
who can possibly save a wretch like me.
Jesus, can you remember me
when You come into Your kingdom?"

Jesus, can you remember me? David thought. *My senseless searching for the right answers, the perfect way to run my life, a clear set of principles to live and work by . . . they all now seem no less than a self-centered set of values to lord over other people. I knew nothing. I had no clue what life was really about. Joani had once called me the last principled man on earth. She was only partially right. I was a principled man, but probably not the last one on the earth. I was better suited to be called the lost principled man. I have thought that the true adventure of life would be captured in being a good man, in living by right standards. I realize tonight that I've been a fool.*

What are these other seventy thousand men doing at this stadium? Jesus is speaking through the boxer directly to me.

The boxer lifted the second cross into place—again with the help of another man, but this time with greater effort. These were not hollow props, but actual trees, thick-cut raw trees, heavy, burdensome. As heavy as the burdens that the characters the actor was portraying were carrying.

He threw down his white skullcap and put a crown of thorns on his head as he shuffled toward the third cross—the one in the middle. Confusion engulfed his face. *Did thorns actually pierce his forehead?* David asked himself. *Is that blood on his face?*

The tall beam was braced three feet in the air at one end. It was longer than the other two center poles, and the crossbeam was larger, too. However, neither one had been precut like the previous ones. He picked up the crossbeam, leaned it on the center pole, and then grabbed an ax.

"Yes, I will remember."

He took a hard swing at the middle of the crossbeam with the ax. The pieces flew. He took another swing and another and another.

"Your faith has found a home in my heart.
I came to this earth to pay for a sin
that you yourself could never pay."

With each swing of the ax, and each splinter of wood that flew from the cross, David envisioned the layers of hardness enclosing his heart being chipped away. *I am not a bad person. I am not an unreasonable man. But I am a sinner nonetheless.*

"Let not your heart be troubled.
Believe in God.
Believe also in me.
In my Father's house, there are many mansions.
If it were not so, I would have told you.
For I go to prepare a place for you.
And if I go to prepare a place for you,
I will come again and receive you to myself.
That where I am, you may be also."

The boxer's breathing labored extensively. Occasionally, the blade of his ax would miss its mark and David could feel the pain shoot through his own arms.

"I am the way, the truth, and the life.
No one comes to the Father except through me."

This is where the enormous conviction my father has grasped has originated from. Not from his books or his principles. Not from his goodness or his steadiness or his heritage. Not even from his church or his pastor. His conviction is solidified at the foot of the cross and his personal encounter with Jesus Christ Himself.

The boxer stepped to the opposite side of the beam and began cutting away the remainder of the rough notch in the center of the log.

> *"In my Father's sovereignty,*
> *He planted this tree.*
> *He watered this tree.*
> *He nurtured this tree.*
> *And now in His love for all mankind*
> *and His passion to reconcile the world to Himself,*
> *He turns this tree into a sacrificial altar for you*
> *and for anyone who would believe,*
> *so that you might have life."*

That Bible verse, from Second Corinthians chapter five, kept roaring through David's head. *Therefore, if anyone is in Christ, he is a new creation; the old has gone, the new has come! All this is from God, who reconciled us to himself through Christ.*

> *"No greater love has any man*
> *than to lay down his life for his friends.*
> *And you are my friends*
> *if you do what I command you."*

He finished cutting the rough notch in the crossbeam and laid the ax down. He lifted the beam into place. Exhausted, he picked up three large nails and set about nailing the logs together at the center joint.

*"I no longer call you slaves,
for a slave does not know what his master is doing."*

The hammer fell on the first nail. He struck it again and again until it sank fully into the wood.

*"But I call you friends.
I call you friends!"*

Christ wants to be my friend? I've never been a slave . . . The hammer fell on the second nail. *Yes, I have been a slave—to my own selfish ways. And now, Christ wants to be my friend?*

*"Because everything I've heard from the Father,
I have made known to you."*

The boxer took the third nail and placed it in the wood. He summoned his remaining strength and struck the nail. *Clank! Clank!*

How much of my life has been led by God despite my desire to lead it myself? Did He bring me to this place?

*"Father, glorify now the Son that the Son may glorify thee.
That to whom all thou has given Him,
he may give eternal life.
And this is eternal life—
that they may know Thee,
the only true God
and Your Son whom Thou has sent."*

The boxer's breathing was deep and labored. He braced the cross under his shoulder and pushed it upward. Two men helped this time as the massive middle cross was thrust upright. It was ten feet taller than the other two. The white wood chips were strewn about the stage.

> *"Yes, I'll remember you.*
> *Yes, I'll remember you today.*
> *You shall be with me in paradise."*

Thank you for remembering me, Father. The words rolled over and over in David's head.

> *"Father, you are patient and slow to anger,*
> *not wanting any to perish,*
> *but for all to come to repentance.*
> *Father, forgive these men, for they know not what they do."*

I repent, Father, for my lack of understanding just how great Your love is for me.

> *"I was pierced for their transgressions;*
> *crushed for their iniquities.*
> *The chastening for their well-being*
> *has fallen upon me.*
> *And by my scourgings,*
> *they are healed."*

Your death on the cross has given me life.

> *"My God, my God, why has . . .*
> *why has thou forsaken me?*
> *Where are you, Daddy?*
> *Where's my dad?"*

Jack Freeman's faith could not save his son David. He needed to see Jesus for himself. He needed to stand at the foot of His cross alone. He needed to see his sins nailed there. He needed to know that Jesus died for him. Yes, for the sins of the whole world. But David needed to know that Jesus died for *him*.

"Into thy hands, I commit my spirit."

Lord Jesus, my awesome, incredible God . . . take my life. Let me live for You.

"It is finished."

EIGHTEEN

The boxer removed his crown of thorns while a singer began, "Were You There When They Crucified My Lord." As the boxer wiped the sweat and blood from his rugged face, he said,

"Wherever you look, you will always find three blood-stained crosses standing there, towering high above the earth for all mankind to see. On the cross in the middle there's a Savior with hands pierced and arms outstretched as if to define the broad expanse of God's boundless love. Crucified on the two crosses beside Him were two thieves. Two men condemned to die. Helpless. Hopeless. Caught in a losing battle between flesh and spirit. When it all comes down, the only thing that matters is which side of the cross you're on."

He described the men on each side of the cross of Christ.

Both were in the same position of life and yet one chose to rail at Jesus and the other asked for mercy. The boxer repeated:

"When it all comes down,
the only thing that matters
is which side of the cross you're on."

Tonight, I've seen Jesus from both sides of His cross, David thought. *I've seen Him from the left side, the side where I have lived for most of my life—a judgmental, condescending, religious side where I have reduced God to my human level and tried to form and fashion Him to my style, my likeness, and my size.*

And tonight I've also seen Him from the right side of His cross—the side that offers His love, His grace, His strength, His mercy.

"When it all comes down,
the only thing that matters
is which side of the cross you're on."

But how can I stand in God's presence? How can I approach Him? It's not like approaching my own father, is it?

"One man says, 'God, what can You do for me?'
Another man says, 'God, what can I do for You?'
One man lives to store his treasures on earth.
Another man lives to store his treasures in heaven.
One man lives to gain it all.
Another man lives to give it all away.
One man lives for men.
Another man lives for God.
When it all comes down,
the only thing that matters
is which side of the cross you're on."

David tried to fathom how much had overwhelmed his heart in such a short time. The weekend was a little less than two hours old, and already he was astounded beyond his imagination.

> *"One man sees his lost friends perishing*
> *and passes them indifferently.*
> *Another man sees his lost friends perishing,*
> *and leads them to the right hand of God."*

The boxer went on to relate his battle with cancer and the slim chances the doctors had given him to live. He continued to struggle with the uncertainties of what each new day would bring, he told the audience.

> *"We all have our public self that everybody can see.*
> *And then we all have our private self*
> *that only our wife or our closest friend can see.*
> *But then we have our personal self*
> *that only God and us can see.*
> *Pretty much everyone is caught in the middle*
> *of the drama as to which side of the cross you're on."*

David was surprised this speaker believed that most men were also going through the same struggles he was going through. David thought he was the only one. Part of that was caused by his own self-centeredness, but part of the reason was because the struggle was so personal to him. And God had reached into the deepest parts of his soul tonight and revealed the truth of his life.

The boxer related a story of a football player named Jim who had been an abused child. He referred to him as a "product of a trans-generational curse that a lot of us in here are a product of." David couldn't relate. His childhood had been wonderful, nothing out of the ordinary. He knew his father and the love of his father, too.

"But one night a speaker came by Arizona State University and Jim had a collision with the cross."

A collision with the cross—that I can relate to, David thought.

"Not knowing what he was doing, Jim gave his heart to Jesus Christ because surely, he thought, I need a dad. I've never had one."

Thank God I've had a dad, a great dad. I wish he was right here in front of me so I could thank him personally.

"When it all comes down, the only thing that matters is which side of the cross you're on."

The boxer related other stories of men who were filled with so much pain and hurt that the only way they knew how to respond was to drown their pain and hurt with alcohol or drugs or pornography. He described men who had wealth and power, but were empty on the inside, and men who were filled with rage and anger.

"Nobody at Promise Keepers would ever come out and condemn anyone—we've been there. We know the pain. We know the emptiness."

David's pain was the realization that he could not make it on his own. His hurt was realizing that his principles could not sustain him in his daily life. His rage was in his thinking how foolish and self-centered he'd been.

"What the thief on the right
and these men have in common
is that they were willing to bring
whatever it was that separated them from Christ
and lay it at the foot of the cross,
humbly before God."

Whatever separates me from Christ? Once again, David remembered that verse: "If a man is in Christ, he is a new creation."

"The thief on the cross had nothing to bring
except his faith in Jesus."

I have nothing to bring either, Lord. Except my faith that You are my Savior.

"So much of evangelism today is cheap and easy.
We get enough religion in us to last us
four or five days down the line."

Not me. I'm a new creation. And again: "The old has passed away. The new has come."

"What we need is a regime change;
a change of leadership.
We don't need another pep talk.
We need a change of leadership."

A pep talk? Is that all this is? A small crack in the door, and doubt had crept into David's heart. **"You're just getting emotional. What you're feeling isn't real. It's all brainwashing and theatrics."**

"Salvation is cardiac revolution.
Salvation is full committal."

"But you're a good man. You go to church. You pray. Why the sudden change in your emotional approach to your religion?"

"When it all comes down,
the only thing that matters
is which side of the cross you're on."

"There's a commitment process to this? You're not up for that. That's not part of your makeup. You're already a firm believer: in your principles, your good principles, based on solid thought. Not this emotionalism being thrown in your face."

"Your fruit will not save you.
You'll be saved only by grace.
When true salvation takes place,
when you take those steps
from the left side of the cross
to the right side of the cross
and you ask Him to fill your heart,
then you will be saved."

"Saved? Saved from what? There's no safety in that cross. It will only bring you pain and discomfort. I'll see to that."

"Your Father cares for you.
He sent His Son Jesus to die for you."

"You already know that. It's no big deal."

*"If there's anyone who doesn't know
the Father's love like that...
If that's the love you've been seeking . . . "*

"There's no need to seek. You've already found your beliefs in your principles."

*"No matter where you come from . . .
No matter what you've done . . ."*

"You're not a bad man. You're a whole lot better than those people on those talk shows, than that woman at the Burger Royal, than Mr. and Mrs. Rantoul—and especially better than that poor, pathetic girl, that Joani Givens."

"The ground is level at the foot of the cross."

"Words, rhetoric, drama."

"This is not a whim or a momentary reaction."

"Yes, it is."

*"And if it is your desire to make
the toughest commitment a man could ever make,
I'm going to invite you to become
what the Bible calls a bondservant of Christ."*

"You're not a slave."

*"A bondservant was a man
who loved his master so much
that even though he was free,
he would chain his heart back to his master."*

"A free slave? Rhetoric."

"Second Chronicles sixteen, nine says,
'For the eyes of the Lord range throughout the earth
to strengthen those whose hearts are fully committed to Him.'
If you are willing to give
whatever has separated you from Christ -
your anger,
your hatred,
your pain . . . "

"You have none of those in your life."

"Your bitterness,
your lack of faith . . . "

"None of those, either."

"If you are willing to give
whatever has separated you from Christ . . . "

"You already have that."

" . . . and willing to say
'Lord Jesus, I receive you into my heart tonight
as my Lord and Savior.
I want a regime change in my life,'
then I'm going to ask you to come forward
and make an unwavering,
uncompromising,
unprecedented
commitment of your life
to Jesus Christ."

"Go forward? How emotionally coercive."

*"Let's stand together
and pray together as a family
as the Lord assures us of our salvation."*

David stayed seated, folded his hands, and buried his face inside of them. He hoped for appearance's sake that everyone around him would leave him alone because they thought he was praying. But he was actually trying to hide from the doubt in his mind—and the reality taking place around him.

NINETEEN

David felt no joy for those men who had gone forward. He sided with the voice in his head that said they were responding to religious emotionalism, rhetoric, and theatrics. Yet he also believed that the voice was only whispering a portion of the truth, so he took hold of the hope that the *whole* truth was somewhere out there in the arena, even though he was still waffling on pledging his heart to seizing that truth and responding to it.

After a few minutes of sitting with his head in his hands, David stood up and tried to blend in with the others around him. Some men were singing. Some were praying. A couple of guys from David's group had actually gone forward. One man from his church group looked over at him, smiled, and said, "Isn't this incredible?"

"Yes," David responded, but it was clear that he was still

sorting it all out. He noticed several men were heading toward the outer concourse of the area, so he made a move in that direction as well, to see if he could find a restroom.

The crowd was buzzing with conversation. Groups of men were hugging and congratulating men who had gone forward. Several were huddled in prayer. The band was playing in the background as men were still gathering at the front of the arena to pray with counselors. David was physically part of the exhilaration of the event, but he felt isolated from the spirit of the gathering. He made his way to the bathroom. It was crowded like it is at any big sporting event. He waited in line for several minutes and avoided eye contact as best as he could.

As he washed his hands, he caught a glimpse of his face in the mirror. Normally he looked at his face to observe his appearance. This time he looked into his soul.

Where are you going with this, David? he thought. *What does all this mean for your life?* That little voice of doubt still haunted him. **"Steady yourself, David. You'll get through this. Then you can return to the safety of your principled life."**

He splashed water on his face and looked into his eyes, hoping to be able to interpret the significance of the moment. As the droplets of water dripped off his skin, he prayed, "God, help me see the truth."

He performed the simple task of wiping his face off with a paper towel, and suddenly and unceremoniously, he saw the truth. The voice was wrong! There was nothing steady in his life if he was living with doubt or fear. And there was no safety in living a principled life, especially if those principles were only based on *David Freeman's* observations and experiences. His doubts and fears, which were as transparent as the water on his face, could only be absorbed and removed by the truth of Christ. He needed to find out more about this "living for Christ."

Therefore, if anyone is in Christ,
he is a new creation;
the old has gone,
the new has come!

David tossed the paper towel into the wastebasket and turned to go back into the arena and join the group from his church and the 70,000 Promise Keepers. The truth of living a life in Christ was in that arena, and he needed to hear what God had to say to him.

As he entered the arena and made his way back to his seat, another speaker was already at the podium. A soft-spoken man with a slight southern accent was telling a story. As he gave the punch line—something about a dog being chained to an old engine block—the crowd roared with laughter. He said, "There is a moral to this story. What are you chained to tonight? If it's going down, so are you. But if it's staying up, then you're staying up, too. What are you chained to?"

That was a good question. David looked in his program and read that the speaker was James Ryle from Tennessee. He was the head of Truth Works Ministries. I need some truth, he thought, so he settled in to listen to what Ryle had to say.

"Psalm 142, verse 7 says, 'Set me free from my prison,
that I might praise Your name.' The interesting thing
about that verse is that there is no record in Scripture or
history that David was ever in prison. He is speaking of
those things that restrict and limit us from reaching our full
potential as God intended for us to do."

I am rich with potential, but as I told—well, really con-
fessed—to Pastor John and his brother Paul, I am missing some-
thing.

*"You might be saying, 'Something's holding me back.
Something's keeping me from fully expressing myself as You
created me to be. And I need You, Jesus, to set me free so that I
can go the distance and give You everything You're worth.'"*

I need You, Jesus, to set me free from my doubts and fears.

*"There's nothing in this world as magnificent as a man who is
forgiven, free, and filled with the Holy Spirit. Brother, what in
the world is keeping you from being that guy? Whatever it is,
it's not worth it. And it's deceiving you into thinking that it has
the power to keep you back."*

"David, it's thinking like *this* that will hold you back."
"Enough!" David prayed, quietly, but out loud. "Lord, take
this doubt from me. That's what's keeping me from being the
man You want me to be."

*"Jesus came to do something about this dilemma.
He said, 'I have come that you might have life, and that
you might have it more abundantly.' We cannot go through our
same old routines and expect that we're going to make
any substantial differences in our lives."*

I am the master of useless routines.

*"It's time for us
to trust an extraordinary God
to make us extraordinary men
in these extraordinary times."*

There is something more. *"Always something more,"* as Pastor
Brunette had said. *There are no levels of assurance to my salvation. It's an either/or situation. But there are other levels in my*

walk with Him. I am sure He is calling me to that next level of commitment.

"Jesus said, 'I am the way, the truth, and the life.
No one comes to the Father, except through me.'
He is the way that you might be saved;
the truth that you might sure;
and He is the life that you might be satisfied.

Let me ask you this, men:
Are you saved?"

Yes.

"Are you sure?"

Yes.

"Are you satisfied?"

No. But now I know where I can find that satisfaction.

James went on to describe how, at nineteen, he found himself in prison wondering what would become of his life. He had stumbled on a Bible verse that said, "All things work together for good to those who love God and are called according to His purpose."

"Men, somehow I knew God had a call on my life
and that if I said yes to Him,
that He'd work all this out
in a way that would blow my mind.
And He's got the same proposition for you."

I can't work this out for myself. Only God can work this out.

"What is your prison?
What is it that's keeping you
from walking in forgiveness
and freedom
and the fullness of the Spirit of God?"

That's easy. It's my principles that are based on my own rea-
soning instead of hearing God's voice and letting Him develop
my convictions.

*"Some men say it's **guilt**.*
You've done something
that you can't get forgiveness for.
Something so bad you think
even God won't let you off the hook.

*Maybe it's **shame**.*
Shame: not because of something you did,
but because of something done to you.

*Some are in prison by **fear**.*
You want to believe.
You want to trust.
You want to step out.
But you're afraid of rejection
or you're afraid of failing
or you're afraid of getting it wrong.

Or maybe it's pride."

That's it. It's my pride.

"Like you've got it handled.
Maybe you don't see yourself as a thief,

but you're a good man.
We think that being good gets us closer to God.
Our goodness takes us away from God
if we think our goodness will earn God's favor.
In fact, goodness makes us worse
because it makes us think
that we're better than everybody else."

My goodness can't earn me God's favor, David told himself. *I knew that all along, but I've chosen not to live by it. This has shot right to my heart. It's the truth I needed to hear.*

James went on to relate Bible stories of the prodigal son and the man with the withered hand. However, David had already heard the message that he needed to hear. His pride in living a principled life based on his goodness, and his judging of other people by his standards, was not a God-pleasing way to run his life. David desired a complete change of thinking and an unconditional release from his prison of pride, principles, and a judgmental heart. *This is where my healing needs to take place.*

"Jesus said to the guy with a withered hand,
'Stand up' and 'come forward.'
The Pharisees didn't care about Jesus
healing the man's hand.
They were only concerned
about what the law said."

I've been a Pharisee. I've only cared about how people behaved. How they acted. Which side of the tracks they grew up on. How they lived up—or didn't live up—to my standards.

"Then Jesus said,
'Stretch forth your hand,'

*and this man did
what he did not have the ability to do
before Jesus stepped into his life.
He reached his potential.
He stretched forth his hand."*

*I need to be that guy. I need to stretch out my hand to Jesus
and do what I can't do on my own: let Him lead my life.*

*"From the moment Jesus broke that Sabbath law
and set these Pharisees spinning off in anger,
it was only a matter of time
until they put Him on the cross.
Sin is why Jesus died on the cross,
but it was religion that hammered the nails in His hands."*

*Stand up. Come forward and stretch out your hand. Maybe
that's what I need to do.*

"Does Jesus see here tonight in this place a Pharisee?"

Yes. Oh, God, yes.

*"I know I'm going at you hard, brother,
but some of you are so bound up
in the belief that how you behave
is going to get you acceptance with God.
There is only one thing that gets us into heaven
and that is this: Jesus paid it all.*

*Nothing in my hand I bring.
Simply to thy cross I cling."*

James asked everyone to bow their heads for prayer. This

time David wasn't faking it.

> *"Lord, set these men free*
> *from that prison of bondage,*
> *and let them become devout men*
> *who are true with integrity*
> *and faithfulness*
> *and uncompromising conviction.*
> *And let them be likable, lovable guys*
> *who give the people they meet*
> *a chance to see Jesus, too."*

Lord, that's my prayer right now. Help me to be free. I know I'm forgiven. I know I'm saved. But help me to be free to live as You would want me to live.

> *"Guys, I want to ask you to take a bold step*
> *if the Lord is dealing with you right now*
> *and you want to walk out of that prison."*

This is where that voice of doubt had crept in before. The Lord was dealing with David. He wanted to take that bold step, but it was so out of his character.

> *"Here's what Jesus said*
> *to the man with the withered hand:*
> *'Stand up.*
> *Step forward.*
> *And stretch out your hand.'*
> *We want to pray for you.*
> *Come forward tonight.*
> *You're getting out of prison—*
> *tonight."*

David folded his hands and prayed. "Lord, release me from the prison of my pride. Help me to live for You as a man of conviction."

Men were walking forward to pray with counselors. It still felt awkward to David, though. He'd only seen this kind of thing done at rallies on television. The church he attended didn't do anything like this. He had always thought it was too emotional and that it leaned more toward the dramatic instead of the sincere. "Lord, tell me what You want me to do," David prayed quietly.

"Some of you are hedging.
You're holding back because of fear or doubt.
Guys, whatever it is that's keeping you
from being forgiven,
free,
and filled with the Holy Spirit of God—
it's not worth it."

I know. I know. But I don't want to do this only because I'm responding to the drama of the moment.

"Guys, we are in this thing together.
Maybe someone near you needs some help.
Turn to someone near you and say,
'If you need to go forward,
I'll go with you.'"

The room started spinning. David had a deep desire to talk with someone about all of this. It was overwhelming. Men from all sections of the arena had looked at each other as James had suggested and then started flooding toward the podium area in groups of two, men leading men to a public commitment of faith and a recognition of release. *God, how I want to talk with someone.* David felt isolated again. *God, what do you want me to do?*

David looked up and glanced to his left. Amid 70,000 men, all the shapes and sizes and colors of the men in the arena, all the different T-shirts and hats and religious backgrounds, he turned and looked—miraculously, he was sure—directly into the eyes of his dad, sitting across from him about halfway up the lower arena seats a hundred feet away. Jack was looking at David with conviction and understanding, and when he saw that David had caught his eye, he mouthed the words, "If you need to go forward, I'll go with you." David shook his head yes as he pointed toward the stage area, and then started heading to the aisle to go forward.

They met on the floor off to the side of the stage. "Dad, do I *have* to do this?"

"No, Son, you don't. But do you want to?"

"I think I need to. I just need to."

They prayed and talked with a trained counselor. David confessed his pride at thinking he could run his own life and then talked of his desire to turn his life over to God's control. The counselor assured him that his walk with Christ would be a "one step at a time" process, and that this was only the first step. He said that tomorrow's sessions would be very helpful in showing him some practical paths to take regarding his prayer life, daily quiet time in God's Word, and fellowship with other believers. He congratulated David on having the courage to answer God's call and told him he would keep him in his prayers.

Jack and David huddled off to the side as the praise band led the conference in singing "Man of the Spirit, Man of the Word."

"Dad, thanks for all your help . . . all your prayers . . . for encouraging me to come here this weekend."

"I wanted you to experience what I'd experienced. I knew if

the Lord could touch me, that He could touch you, too.

"How can I put all this into words, Dad? What's next?"

"Like the counselor said, David, you're going to have to take this a step at a time. Maybe you'll get some tips from the sessions tomorrow. Let's enjoy tonight."

"Good idea."

* * * * *

The flunky waited nervously in the car. He hadn't heard a sound from the farmhouse for nearly twenty minutes. That had to be good news. Or it could be bad news. He didn't know what to think.

No other cars had come down the dirt country road since he'd let Snake out to move on the farmhouse. The flunky sat with the window rolled down and listened to the night sounds of the open country, imagining all the possibilities.

Suddenly, he heard a screen door and the sound of people arguing. "Joani, don't go. Please!" begged a woman. Snake shouted back an obscenity. The flunky could barely make out the figures standing on the front porch as he heard the garage door lift open. He heard a car start and then saw red and white tail lights as the car backed out of the garage and turned toward the driveway. He squinted and held his hand up to shield his eyes from the sudden brightness of the headlights coming toward him since his eyes had become adjusted to the darkness. The black Camaro drove beside the flunky's car and skidded to a stop on the dirt.

"Don't need you anymore tonight," Snake shouted over the rough idling of the Camaro. "Got what I came for. I'll give you a call."

"OK, Snake. Yeah, you give me a call if you need me," the flunky responded as Snake showed an indifferent expression. He could see Joani sitting on the passenger side, facing forward with her chin lowered to her chest. Snake took off down the road, kicking up dust that swirled in through the open window.

"Dis ain't worth it," the flunky muttered to no one but himself as he started his car. And then, he answered himself. "Yeah, but what else you got goin' for ya?"

June and Herb held each other on the porch and prayed as the Camaro drove off down the driveway and east down the road, back toward St. Louis. They saw a second car at the end of their driveway take off in the opposite direction.

"Lord, what can we do?" June prayed quietly, with Herb listening. "What can we do? We need a miracle, Lord. We need a miracle."

TWENTY

The second day of the gathering was more informative and less emotionally charged. The music was powerful. The speakers were dynamic. However, the messages were centered on practical ways for a man to grow in his personal faith, in his relationship with his wife and family, and with other men of faith. David took notes and was able to talk over most of the material with Pastor John, who was looking forward to getting together with the men from church when they got back to St. Louis. David felt like he was seeing everything spiritual in his life from a whole new perspective.

Jack and David had lunch together the second day. They sat with their respective church groups in the same general areas for the Saturday sessions as they did for Friday night. Jack approached David just before the lunch break, where 70,000 men were served a sack lunch in less than half an hour.

Men sat all around the arena area, inside and out. Jack and

David found a place to sit on a concrete wall in the shade just outside the stadium. It was a warm, sunny day in Indianapolis, and the shade made their time outside favorable for a conversation of some depth and meaning.

"I'm really learning a lot, Dad. I can't believe how clear the idea of living for Christ seems to me now. It's like night and day. I came here believing in God and thought that if I did all the right things that were expected of me, that I'd find enjoyment and fulfillment. Now I find out that it's Christ living in me that matters more. What's next?"

"Who knows?"

"'Who knows'? I thought you've been through all this, and you've found all the answers."

"I'm not God, David. I'm your Dad. I don't know all the answers. But God does."

"But can't you give me a hint of what I need to do next?" David asked.

"David, you need to stop trying to figure out what to *do*, and spend some time getting to know God. He'll let you know where you're supposed to go and what you're supposed to do."

"Yeah, but I want to know how to fit this into my day."

Jack laughed. "David, you're such a perfectionist. You've lived life so long by your day-timer that you can't fathom the idea of going with the flow. Remember what that speaker said this morning about spending a quiet time with God every day. I thought of you when he said there will be guys who will be determined to try and read the Bible completely through in a year by scheduling a slot in their schedule to read four chapters a day. There's only a select few guys with the temperament to do that."

David admitted to Jack that he had thought about that "reading the Bible in a year" plan and had even made a mental note to check that out when he got home. "That's me, I guess."

"I know, Son. But if you only concentrate on a 'four chapters per day' reading plan you might miss some of the 'nuggets' he referred to."

The speaker had talked about spending time going over a short section of the Bible, say fifteen or twenty verses or one short chapter, and grabbing out selected "nuggets" of wisdom that God would use to teach something important for that day. He called it "meditating on God's word."

Jack grasped his Bible firmly, held it out to David, and said, "Meditating on the Word and letting it speak to you *that day* is a lot for any of us to handle. This book speaks volumes in such short verses. We need to grab the nuggets. You get enough nuggets and you'll be rich."

That made sense to David. He knew it was going to take some time for him to change his thinking patterns, but he looked forward to the process.

They ate their lunch, enjoying friendly conversation. After a slight lull in the dialogue, David asked his dad, "You think this change God has brought about in my life has any implications toward that girl I told you all about a few weeks back?"

Jack gave him a fatherly smile and said, "Like I told you, Son, I'm not God. You're going to have to ask Him about that. But you might want to first tackle a smaller problem than love—like world peace or the global economy."

"Love's a challenge, huh?"

"Yeah, love's a challenge. It's worth pursuing, but it is a challenge."

They gathered up their things and got ready to head back into the arena for the afternoon sessions.

"By the way, David, speaking of challenges . . . you remember the Mrs. Rantoul incident I reminded you about when we went to the Cubs game?"

"Sure, what about it?"

"Did you ever think it was curious that you got a call from your supervisor about umpiring the next night for that same team?"

"Did *you* have something to do with that?"

"I made a little call to your supervisor and suggested it might be good for you to get back on the horse right away."

"*You* did that?"

"Yeah, and I can't even try to shift the blame to your mother. She wanted to go and punch Mrs. Rantoul's lights out. I thought it might be better to have you face the challenge of umpiring another game with them right away rather than see your mother get arrested for assault."

"I'm learning more stuff about you every day, Dad."

"It's getting tougher all the time to stay ahead of you. But I'm trying my best."

"You *are* the best, Dad."

"I think you're pretty special too, Son."

* * * * *

David spent the next couple of weeks developing a quiet time of reading various sections of the Bible and meditating on what God was specifically showing him in His Word. His prayer life started progressing from merely thanking God for the "stuff" he had in his life to asking God to show him what He wanted him to do and where He wanted him to go. It didn't take too long for David to be eager about spending that time in prayer and in the Bible each day. He watched a lot less television and didn't miss it at all.

On a business trip toward Memphis two weeks after the Promise Keepers gathering, David saw a black Camaro on the road. It reminded him of Joani, and he started praying to God for guidance about whether He wanted him to find out how she was doing.

* * * * *

Joani Givens walked into the Alibi Bar with a sober, disconsolate look on her face. She was starting back to work at the miserable St. Louis tavern only one day after her return from her brief escape to the farm near Fair Grove. Carla Harmon, another barmaid at the Alibi and one of Joani's only female friends, was wiping down the bar when Joani entered. Carla's face brightened as she saw her friend, who had been gone from the neighborhood for over a month.

"Joani," Carla called out, "I heard you were back. Good to see you."

"What's so good about it?" Joani muttered.

Carla's expression changed from joy to sad concern at Joani's remark. "I just thought . . . "

"You just thought *what*?" Joani glared at Carla with an inner anger that shot right through her.

"I just thought it was good to see you," Carla said hesitantly.

Joani's face took on a calmer expression and she half-smiled at Carla. "I'm sorry, Carla. It's good to see you, too." The two embraced. "It's this place, and Snake, and that dump I'm living in . . . and my life. It's . . . hopeless."

"'Least you got your health," Carla said in a weak attempt at a joke.

Joani could only muster another half-smile. That was all Carla's attempt at humor was worth for now.

TWENTY-ONE

"Lord, I'm wondering what to do about Joani," David prayed. "I've begun to realize that things don't happen by accident to believers—that all things work together for good for those who love You and are called according to Your purpose. I pray You'll show me what to do about Joani. Amen."

David opened his Bible that morning and thought about reading one of the gospel accounts of the life of Jesus instead of one of the other New Testament sections. He had already read several Psalms, mostly at night before he went to bed, but he had decided to stay away from some of the more complicated Old Testament books and also the book of Revelation until he was able to understand more about Jesus Himself. An older gentleman at his church made the comment about Revelation that "these are no bedtime stories." The concerned look on his face was enough to steer David away from that book for now.

He paged through Matthew and settled in on Mark. It got right into the life of Jesus from the time He was baptized. The paragraph headings pointed toward the miracles that Jesus performed, His dealing with the disciples, and the parables He told. David settled in on "The Healing of a Demon-Possessed Man" in Mark chapter 5. Jesus sent the demons from a man named Legion into a herd of pigs, and the herd of pigs ran down into the lake and drowned. He remembered the story from a Sunday School class years ago. The speaker that day was one of the actors from the movie *Jesus*. He told the story of how hard it was in making the movie to get pigs to run as a herd in one direction, and what the production staff did to make that happen.

After the man named Legion was delivered from the demons, he begged Jesus to let him go with Him. David read, "Jesus did not let him, but said, 'Go home to your family and friends and tell them how much the Lord has done for you, and how he has had compassion on you.'" Those words flew off the page at David! It sounded so simple and so directed toward him. He had already told his family about his experience at the Promise Keepers weekend, and now he could sense that the Lord was telling him that he was supposed to tell Joani about how much the Lord had done for him.

As he prayed about it over the next few days, he tried to get it straight in his own mind as to how he should approach her. Admittedly, he had harbored thoughts of a possible love connection, but the more he prayed, the more he knew the Lord was leading him to approach her only as a friend. It was obvious that with her past still haunting her, her living with Snake, and her problem with alcohol, she had more than enough on her plate. Dealing with a closer relationship with David would not enhance her life, but only complicate it further.

David prayed with several of his Promise Keeper friends

at church and with Pastor John, and then felt he was ready to take this next step in the Joani Givens adventure. He prayed, "Lord, give me the right words to say to help communicate to Joani how wrong I was for judging her and turning my back on her. Lord, help me to share what Christ has done for me in the past month and also the reality of what He can do for her." He was scheduled for his quarterly sales trip to Oklahoma on Monday, and he decided to take the time to stop by the farm near Fair Grove.

* * * * *

As David drove down I-44 and got closer to the Waynesville exit where he had his Burger Royal incident some time back, he had the unmistakable notion that he was supposed to pull off, go back to the restaurant, and apologize to the woman he barked at. It was such an unmistakably strong feeling that he couldn't ignore it.

David parked his car at the restaurant and went inside, not knowing exactly what he would say or even if the woman was still working there. There was no one in line as he walked in the door and only a couple of tables were occupied. A teenage girl was at the register and greeted him with, "Hello. Welcome to Burger Royal. May I take your order?"

David stuttered as he looked at the menu on the wall behind the counter because he wasn't really interested in ordering any food; he was here for another purpose. "Uh, yeah," he mumbled. "Just a drink, a large drink. That's good."

"One large drink. That'll be one dollar and twenty-nine cents." He gave the girl two dollars and looked around toward the back to see if the older woman might be working today. The girl handed him a cup and a lid so he could get his drink at the self-service island, and then she handed him his change and a receipt. "Seventy-one cents change and your receipt.

Can I get you anything else?"

He *almost* said, "Yeah, you got an older lady who works here who has trouble counting change?" but he caught himself. "No, thanks," he said, shuffling his feet and looking around. "Just the drink."

David grabbed the cup and turned toward the drink island when the older woman walked around from the back and placed several wrapped packages of napkins on the counter right in front of him. It was her, no doubt about it. David approached her and said, "Ma'am, can I talk to you for a second?"

She looked surprised, but said, "Sure."

"I don't know if you remember me, but I was in here a month or so ago, maybe two months. And I had some trouble getting the right change from my order."

Now the woman looked surprised and confused. "No, I don't think I remember you."

"Well, I spoke kind of rudely to you, and it's been bothering me, and I wanted to come back here in hopes I would see you again and apologize for being so rude to you."

A smile came over the woman's face, brightening her natural complexion. "Well, that's very nice of you, but I really don't remember."

"That's OK. *I* remembered, and I wanted to tell you I was sorry."

"OK. Sure. Yes, that's very nice of you."

David lifted his glass and said, "Well, I gotta go."

"OK. You have a nice day."

"You too."

David filled his glass at the self-service island. It felt like everyone was staring at him, but it was such a different emotion than the one that had gripped him the last time he was in the restaurant. He walked out and smiled again at the older woman and the teenage girl at the register. David knew he had done the right thing.

Rose Hattendorf, a 62-year-old woman who had worked full-time at the Burger Royal in Waynesville for the past two years to make ends meet after her husband had suddenly died, stared at the young man as he walked from the restaurant with his large drink in hand. As the door swung closed behind him, she glanced at Becky, the 16-year-old girl at the cash register, and said, "Now there's something you don't see every day." Becky smiled and giggled as Rose began picking up her packages of napkins. "That's the first one of those . . . I've ever had."

David passed the Lebanon exit where the Gas Stop encounter had happened. Then he passed the rest area where he had met up with Joani. As he came upon the exit where Joani had stashed her Camaro, he briefly thought about stopping to see if the car was still there. But that didn't seem necessary now, so he drove ahead, toward the Fair Grove exit. Besides, it was getting close to sunset, and he didn't want to arrive at the farm after dark.

The scenery along the roads to the farm appeared to boast in its seemingly unchanging color. That was one of the unique characteristics of life in the country. It seemed to shun the intense, extreme, and almost daily reconstruction that city life reveled in.

As David drove down the driveway toward the white farmhouse with the rocking chairs on the porch, he became nervous about what he would say to Joani. "Lord, help me to say the right things. Help me to spend all my time apologizing for my running out on her and not on making excuses for the way I acted. Help her to understand I only want what's best for her. . . . And help me to loosen up."

David stopped his car in the circle drive and started walking down the path to the front porch. Herb's gruff voice barked at him from inside the front door. "Stop right there! Who are you?"

David stopped dead in his tracks. "I'm David Freeman

. . . . Joani's friend? I came by here and met you all a month or so ago."

"It's that David Freeman, Herb. Put that away." It was Aunt June's voice also coming from inside the house. She opened the screen door and came out to greet David, who saw Herb lean a rifle against the inside wall next to the door and then follow June onto the porch as well.

"David, what a surprise to see you. I hope we didn't startle you," June said.

"No. Well, yes, kind of," he stuttered.

"Sorry about that, Mr. Freeman," Herb said. "We're a little skittish around here since . . . well, it's a long story." He turned to June. "Why don't you get us all something to drink and we'll talk with Mr. Freeman."

"Good idea," June said as she hustled back into the house.

"Sit here, David," Herb said as he motioned David toward one of the rocking chairs. David took a seat. "Like I said, we're a little skittish around here lately. You see, Joani left to go back to St. Louis with that . . . that criminal roommate of hers. Couple weeks ago now it was. He came after dark and surprised us all. I saw he was carrying a pistol in his belt. He never brought it out, but we weren't going to give him reason to use it. Looked like she just gave up and went back with him."

June came back out onto the porch with two glasses of lemonade and offered them to Herb and David. David held on to his, but Herb set his down on the wood flooring. "Joani's not here, David," she said as she sat down in the chair next to Herb.

"I told him that already."

"She went back to St. Louis," June said.

"I told him that, too."

"Well, what haven't you told him, Herb?"

Herb turned back to David. "We thought she might be makin' a turn for the better, like she was finally rid of that guy and ready to move on. We went and retrieved her car, and she got a job at a local hangout to try and raise some money."

"But then she'd go and spend half her money on booze. That alcohol has a hold on her," June said as she started to cry, pulling a handkerchief out of her dress pocket and dabbing her eyes.

"She went back with him?" David asked, stunned.

"When he showed up and surprised us all, she looked so shocked like it knocked all the wind out of her sails, and she just gave up. It was like she didn't want to run anymore."

"Wasn't she scared of him?" David probed.

"Not enough to matter, I guess," Herb said. "He mentioned something to her about knowing too much, but then he kind of sweet-talked her. She got so down and out that she didn't care anymore."

"She misses her mom real bad," June said. "She seemed like she lost all hope about really makin' something out of her life when that . . . that *devil* showed up. It was the alcohol talkin' to her," she said sternly.

"Have you spoken with her since she went back?"

"A couple of times," Herb said. "She told us not to bother anymore. Said she'd be OK and not to worry."

June butted in. "Then one time that . . . that guy she's with took the phone away from her and threatened Herb and me. Said we better quit calling or he'd do something about it 'cause he knows where we live. I know he knows someone else in the area 'cause the night she went back with him, we saw another car at the end of the driveway drive away as they left."

"We called the police," Herb added, "but they said there wasn't anything they could do because she went back with him of her own free will. It wasn't like she was kidnapped or anything. I swear I don't know what this world's comin' to."

The situation was more serious than David had ever imagined it would be. The verse from Mark five came back to him.

*"Go home to your family and friends
and tell them how much the Lord has done for you,
and how he has had compassion on you."*

"I've got to tell you—a lot has happened to me in the past couple of months, too. Nothing like what's happened to you all or Joani, but I've had my eyes opened to a new way of life . . . in Christ."

June flipped her hands into the air and said, "Praise the Lord." Herb had a more cautious look on his face.

"You haven't become one of those Bible thumpers—those fanatics that are so heavenly minded they're no earthly good, have you?" Herb asked.

"No, sir. But I have turned my life over to Jesus, and I'm listening to Him and letting Him run my life instead of relying on my own instincts."

"Well, that sounds good. I'm happy for you," Herb said. But he still didn't look like he was convinced David was going to be much help to Joani.

An overwhelming wave of conviction came over David. "I tell you what I'll do. I'll try to get in touch with Joani when I get back to St. Louis on Friday. I don't know what I can say to her, but maybe I can show her how much you all care about her . . . and that she could have something to live for if she just looked for it . . . and maybe that her mother wouldn't have wanted her to go down the road she's going." David was making all this up on the fly, but it kept sounding better the more he thought through it.

"Don't be afraid to tell her how much God loves her, David," June added in a calm, caring voice. David nodded.

"You make sure you stay away from that criminal guy she's with," Herb said. "I don't want you gettin' hurt tryin' to do something for Joani."

"And don't call her at home," June insisted. "I've got the

number of that bar she works at. Maybe you can call her there and meet her somewhere. Oh, I hope she'll listen to you, David."

"Well, let's hope I can say something that makes sense to her," David said.

Herb leaned forward. "David, I want to pray for you." They each bowed their heads and folded their hands. "Lord, this young man may be the miracle we prayed for. But he can't do it on his own. We ask You to be with him as he tries to contact Joani, and we pray You open her heart to listen to what he has to say. And we pray your protection on David as he faces this challenge. Be with him, Lord, and give him the strength to do the job. We pray all this in Your name. Amen."

They all lifted their heads and looked at each other. Herb wiped an eye and reached out to shake David's hand. June said, "David, you must come in and have a bite to eat with us."

"Yes," Herb said. "We insist."

"Sounds good to me," David said.

* * * * *

David called Pastor John on his road trip to Oklahoma to ask him to pray regarding David's desire to talk with Joani. He also asked him to have some of the other Promise Keepers pray for him, too. David gave Pastor John enough background information to give him a hint that this situation was a little out of David's league, but that he needed to stretch his faith by putting it into action. David knew God was behind his effort, but he also knew he needed his Christian brothers' prayers, and badly.

David also called his dad and mom to relay the information. They were concerned about his safety, despite the fact David hadn't told them anything about Snake.

"Are you sure you're not getting in over your head, David?" his mom asked.

"I don't know, Mom. The girl is a friend. I care about her. And we all could use a little more 'caring about each other' in this world, right?"

"I guess so, David," his mother said. "I'm just your mother, and I'm always going to worry about you."

"You wouldn't be a mom if you didn't care," David insisted.

* * * * *

On Thursday night David called Joani at the bar from his motel room in Joplin. A grouchy-sounding voice answered: "Alibi Bar."

"I was wondering if Joani Givens is working tonight."

"Joani? Yeah, just a minute," the woman said bluntly.

Joani got on the phone almost immediately. "This is Joani. Who's this?"

"Joani, it's David Freeman."

"Who?"

"David. A couple months ago, I took you to your aunt and uncle's farm."

"Oh, sure," she said matter-of-factly. "Whadda you want?"

"I was wondering if we could get together and talk."

"What for?"

"I want to see how you're doing . . . and just talk."

David could hear the clanking of glasses, and conversation, in the background. "I'm kinda busy right now," Joani said. "I gotta go."

"Can I give you a call or come see you? Do you work to-morrow night?"

"I think I'm working tomorrow. No. I don't know. Look, David, I'm real busy right now. And I don't know if there's any reason we need to talk."

"I stopped by the farm this week. I spoke with June and Herb."

Joani was silent for a few seconds. "Like I said, I don't think there's any reason we need to talk."

"Well, I was going to be back in St. Louis tomorrow night, so I thought I might drop in and see you. OK?"

"It's a free country, David. You do what you want. I gotta go. Good-bye." David heard the click as she hung up. This was obviously going to be more difficult than he could have imagined. And was it worth it?

That was the question he kept asking himself.

* * * * *

Carla Harmon poured drinks from behind the bar for the rowdy patrons at the Alibi. The unusually large Thursday night crowd was in a rambunctious mood. "Who was that?" she asked Joani.

"Some guy. Look, his name is David. He's a . . . guy. He said something about coming by tomorrow. I'm not too wild about seein' him."

"Some guy?" Carla asked.

"Yeah, just some guy," Joani barked over the din of the bar noise.

"Some guy may be coming by to see you?" Carla asked again.

"He may or he may not be coming by. I'm not too wild about seein' him," snapped Joani. "OK?"

"Hey, Joani, get your lazy butt over here and bring us those drinks," yelled a laughing and obviously drunk Snake, who was playing pool with some of the neighborhood sharks.

Carla handed Joani a tray of drinks and held on to it long enough to make Joani look at her. "And this guy who called you is worse than *that*?" She flipped her head in Snake's direction.

"Butt out, Carla," Joani said as she disgustedly tugged the tray of drinks away from her friend, sloshing some of the liquid from the glasses. Joani walked toward the pool tables as Carla shook her head.

* * * * *

"Lord, this doesn't look too promising," David prayed from his room in Joplin, "but I still think I need to visit Joani. Besides, I promised her aunt and uncle that I would. I know I'm going to need Your strength and courage to do this. And I'm going to need Your wisdom to tell me what to say. I feel so inadequate here, but I know this is what You want me to do. Be with me, Lord, and guide me. Please. Amen."

Is all this worth it? David kept repeating to himself. *Is all this worth it? We'll find out tomorrow night. After I get back home to St. Louis, I'll find out where this Alibi Bar is and go down there and find Joani—and try to avoid this 'Snake.'*

TWENTY-TWO

June and Herb folded their hands and bowed their heads as they prayed for their Friday evening meal. " . . . thanking you for this food . . . and Lord, we pray that you be with David Freeman. That he gets a chance to talk with Joani tonight or sometime soon. Amen."

* * * * *

Paul Brunette was in his family room, surrounded by several men from the church who had gathered for a Friday night small group prayer meeting. "Lord, I ask that you be with David Freeman as he counsels a friend of his tonight. Be with him and give him Your strength and guidance."

* * * * *

Pastor John Brunette was in his study at Faith Lutheran Church. It had been a long day and he had tied up all the loose ends of the church's business, but he wanted to spend a few moments in prayer before heading home for dinner. " . . . and Lord, be with David Freeman. He is such an eager servant and wants to do Your will. Be with him as he seeks to minister to his friend Joani."

* * * * *

Sylvia Freeman was washing the Friday evening dinner dishes. She paused for a moment to pray: "Lord be with my son David this evening. Keep him safe."

* * * * *

Jack Freeman was in the living room of his Roselle, Illinois home reading a Christian novel he had recently purchased, but he put it down abruptly as his son David suddenly came to mind. He wasn't sure of the reason why, but he knew he was supposed to pray for David. "God, send your holy angels to surround David tonight. Protect him, Lord."

* * * * *

Sixty-two-year-old Rose Hattendorf sat down by herself to pray for her Friday evening meal of vegetable soup and crackers. She thanked God for the food, the money she'd earned to buy it, and the job that she had that provided that income. " . . . and Lord, be with that nice young man who came in and apologized to me the other day. That was such a bold thing to do. Be with him, Lord."

* * * * *

David parked his car at the corner, right next to the Alibi Bar. The stark difference between this neighborhood and where he lived gave him an edgy, uncomfortable feeling. The sights and the sounds were so unlike his tranquil subdivision. The jukebox inside the bar blared heavy metal noise that carried down the street. A couple of teenagers dressed in black strolled past on the main street. They abruptly stopped talking when they saw David, hesitating in their walk, but they quickly realized that he was no threat to them and they picked up their pace again, continuing their conversation. The green light turned yellow above the intersection as David heard tires screeching away from him a block away on a side street.

David knew he looked out of place as he entered the bar's front door. He saw thuggish bikers playing pool, street hoods guzzling beer and shots, and ladies of the evening laughing at bad jokes told by strangers they had just met. Old, worn-out whiskey posters that had long since outlived their advertising appeal hung loosely on the wall. David was aware that everyone was staring at him, but it was only out of a sense of curiosity that blared, "Who's the clean guy? What's he doing here?" He must have looked unimportant to them, though, because everyone quickly went back to what they were doing once the initial shock of seeing the out-of-place newcomer wore off.

David walked to the bar. A pleasant-faced barmaid with a surprisingly low gruff voice asked him. "Waddaya have?"

"I'm looking for a girl named Joani Givens. I was told she worked here. Is she around?"

"Nah, not tonight. She don't work tonight."

"She said she lived near here. I'm a friend of hers."

"You that guy that called the other night? She said you might come by." She took a quick cleaning swipe at the bar with her towel. David must have looked surprised at her words. "Actually, she said she *didn't* think you'd come by. I'm Carla. You David?" She offered her hand. Three cheap bracelets rattled around her wrist. David obliged and shook her hand cautiously.

"Yes, I'm David. I'd really like to talk with Joani. Do you know where she lives?"

"Yeah, it's just up the side street." She pointed toward the street where David's car was parked. "Third building on the left: apartment 22, second floor."

He smiled and said, "Thanks." As he started to turn, Carla grabbed his arm.

"A little word of advice? Joani's all right. She's a sweet one. But that roommate of hers . . . I'd stay away from him if I was you."

"I've heard that. Thanks for the tip."

"You sure you don't want a drink first?" she asked.

David grinned. "No, thanks."

Carla shook her head and shrugged her shoulders. As David walked away, she muttered, "Good luck, bud. You're gonna need it."

David walked down the dimly lit side street and counted off three buildings. It was solid brick, but about eighty years old. The wear and tear on the building was noticeable. Harsh winters. Blazing hot St. Louis summers. This building had seen its share of history and abuse, but it was still standing despite the disparagement.

David opened the heavy glass and metal front door. No security system in this place. There was an old light on the wall. The dirt accumulated on the frosty covering hindered its illumination. There were about ten steps in front of David to reach the second floor. He grabbed the handrail. It was loose and had gouge marks in it. He let go, thinking he could easily get a splinter in his hand, although that seemed like the least of his worries with each creaking, linoleum-surfaced step he took. David sensed that a sinister figure could spring out at him any second. *People live here?* he thought. *People experience this dread every day?* He prayed, quietly, "Lord, this shouldn't be. No one should have to live like this."

David reached the top of the stairs. The hallway was as dimly lit as the entranceway. The door on the right had two metal numbers nailed to it. The top nail of the two had broken off and the number was hanging down. On the left side of the hall was apartment 22. David took a deep breath and knocked on the door. "God, please be with me."

There was no security peephole in the door. He heard the dead bolt unlock. The door opened slightly. The chain was still attached and pulled tight. Joani recognized David through the open space. She closed the door and unhooked the chain. As she swung the door open and stood there staring at him, she sighed, "What are you doing here?"

* * * * *

Snake and a small-time delinquent dealer were standing in a dimly-lit alleyway. "Where's my money?" growled Snake in a low tone that seemed to echo off the walls of the two abandoned brick buildings on each side of the alley where drug deals were the only enterprise going on these days. The "user" teenager didn't pose much of a threat. Snake merely fixed his imposing stare on the kid, threatening him with severe bodily harm, and the kid immediately coughed over the four hundred dollars he owed Snake with a nervous, sweating hand. "I wasn't holdin' out on ya, Snake," he stuttered.

Snake continued glaring at him while he took the cash. He only looked away from the kid a quick couple of times as he counted the money. It was all there—the whole four hundred. Snake folded it neatly and stuffed it in his pocket. "Don't be late again," he sneered. "I don't wanna have ta . . . lose my temper . . . and get ugly with ya."

The kid gulped and breathed nervously, his heart pounding, as Snake backed away and then turned to get in his car parked at the end of the alleyway.

As Snake drove the twelve blocks back to his neighborhood, he pieced together mental notes on other people who owed him money. He noticed two teenagers hanging out in front of a dingy laundromat. Snake knew them both, and they knew Snake all too well. *They're clean*, he thought. *For now.*

Snake parked the Camaro on the street several doors down from the front of the apartment building where he shared space with Joani. As he walked near the front of his building, he noticed the "Alibi Bar" sign at the end of the block flashing out an invitation. "I need a drink," he muttered to himself. He reached into the front pocket of his jeans and pulled out the neatly folded wad of twenties. "And I got the money to buy a drink," he bragged. He caressed the money between his fingers. "Maybe a bunch of drinks."

Snake walked past the front door of his apartment building. He was still ticked off at Joani for something she'd said or done earlier in the evening. He didn't want her along. He'd see what other, more accommodating company he might scrounge up at the bar. He was so into himself, his money, and his own little world of crime and filth. This was *his* neighborhood. This was *his* turf. *I own that pool table at the Alibi*, he thought.

Almost to the corner, Snake noticed a tan late-model Caprice parked in the street. *Pretty nice car for this neighborhood.*

* * * * *

"Can I come in?" David asked.

"I guess so. How'd you find me?" Joani helped the door swing open, then turned her back on David and walked a couple of steps toward the center of the room.

"I asked someone at the bar. They told me where you lived.

Is Snake . . . "

Joani folded her arms and turned back to face David, interrupting him. "No, he's not here. If he was, you'd've known it by now."

* * * * *

Snake walked triumphantly into the bar. He stopped for a moment at the entrance to make sure everyone noticed him. Pool players lifted their sights from the green cloth to Snake's imposing figure in the door. Several of the players nodded coolly. Snake did own the pool table at the Alibi, as well as the drug traffic in the neighborhood, but these players were into their own brand of tough and didn't want to give Snake the impression he was that much better than them.

Snake stepped up to the bar as Carla the barmaid walked around from the back. Seeing Snake startled her. She assumed that Dave guy must have thought twice about going to Joani's place. Or else Snake had already killed him, and maybe Joani too. "Whaddaya have?" she said to Snake.

Snake reached into his pocket and proudly slapped the four hundred dollars onto the bar, just so he could display it all. "I'll have anything I want," he boasted. "Let's start with a beer."

"Beer it is," said Carla as she grabbed a cold longneck bottle and twisted the cap off. Snake's wad of cash caught the attention of two working girls at a corner booth. They were new to the neighborhood and were not interested in Snake's involvements. They were attracted to his money. The two women looked at each other and smiled slyly. One of them stood and smoothed out her silky red dress. She seemed to communicate, almost telepathically, with her partner as to what their plan of attack would be.

The lady in red sauntered up to the bar a few feet from Snake, far enough away to not seem overly eager and yet close enough to get his attention. Her sweet, scented perfume followed her, and Snake turned his head toward the enticing aroma. She placed one foot seductively on the foot rail and leaned on the bar. "Two beers," she said softly to Carla.

Carla didn't respond verbally, but merely went about getting the beers. She knew what the lady in red's game was.

Snake stared at her long, straight black hair and moved his eyes slowly down her shapely figure to her long legs that sported thin-strapped high-heeled shoes. He started back up the red dress and their eyes met when he got back to her painted face. Her head was turned toward him and she flashed a smile in his direction. Snake liked the attention. He glanced back to the table, where the lady in red's friend was sitting. She smiled too. "I'll take care of those beers, Carla," Snake said as he pushed a twenty across the bar.

"That's very nice of you. Thanks," the lady in red said, attempting to affect a touch of shyness.

"Don't think I've seen you in here before," Snake said.

"We just got in from Indianapolis," she said as she glanced at her friend at the table. The other girl nodded and smiled again. The lady in red stayed perfectly still as Snake inched closer toward her. She was a friendly-faced predator, reeling a Snake into her lair.

"Indianapolis, huh?" Snake responded. "I hear they got cars that go pretty fast in Indy."

"That ain't all the fast things in Indy," she said through a smile. Carla plopped the beers on the counter, startling the lady in red. She glared at Carla, but then smiled sweetly at Snake. "You care to join us?"

"Sounds good to me."

* * * * *

"Is he coming back soon?" David asked Joani.

"Maybe. He didn't say." Her words were brusque, cold.

David looked around at the gloomy apartment. The lighting was dim. The furniture was worn and ragged. There was an old fireplace by the side wall, but it didn't look like a fire had been built in it for some time. "Nice place," David said, trying to break the ice.

"No it's not. Look, what are you here for?"

"I stopped by your aunt and uncle's farm on Monday."

"Did you have fun talking with them? Did they invite you to stay for dinner?" Joani said, still quite curt.

"I stopped by to see *you*."

Joani's temperament lightened, but only a little. "Sorry I wasn't there. I came to my senses and moved back here to paradise. What'd you want to see *me* for?"

"I wanted to talk and . . . apologize for the way I sort of ran out on you the last time I saw you."

"People like to run out on me."

"But there's also a lot of people who care about you."

"Name one," she said.

"Your aunt and uncle are two. Carla at the bar thinks you're OK." Joani shifted her weight to her other foot and stared at David, unconvinced. "And *I* like you. At least, I'd like to be your friend. I did meet you at the rest stop and take you to the farm, didn't I?"

"All right, I got loads of friends, and I'm living in the lap of luxury here at the Taj Mahal. Is that all you wanted to talk to me about?"

"You've developed a lot harder shell than when I last talked to you."

"Yeah, life does that to you sometimes, Dave."

"You still get to choose how you want to live."

"What, are you lecturing me again?"

"No, I'm trying to tell you the truth." Joani thought she'd heard enough and reached out to turn David around and push him toward the door, but he stopped her by grabbing her hand. "Just listen to me for a second." She wriggled free from his grasp and folded her arms again. "I had a change of heart recently. I found out that the way I was leading my life was shallow and empty. I would look at people and judge them instantly by my standards."

"You must have had a field day with me."

"Yeah, I did. But I realized I was wrong. And that's why I wanted to talk with you . . . and apologize for thinking that way about you and deserting you on the farm."

"No big deal, David. You done?"

"No." He stepped closer to her. "I'm no hero. I've got a lot to learn. But I don't believe we got together by chance. That day in Lebanon when I took you to the farm, you said you thought that I might help someone if they were in need. That's what a friend does, and I . . . want to be your friend."

Joani turned and walked away from David. "We're different, David. We don't have anything in common. You're a clean-cut businessman who lives in the suburbs. I'm a waitress in a trashy bar in the city. And don't forget about Snake. He's not going to be happy about this little get-together if he finds out you were the one who helped me get away that day."

David rejected any fear he might have had at dealing with Snake and continued with his knocking on Joani's hard-shelled demeanor. "OK, we're different, but we've both looked hard for some real peace in our lives, and we've both come up empty." Her penetrating eyes made David believe his words were making sense to her. "I've found the way to that peace. It's brought about a change in me, and I'm sure it will work for you, too."

"It's not some self-help guru's motivational tapes, is it?"

"No." He paused. "It's Jesus." Joani sighed and turned away. "It's not church, Joani. It's not religion." Joani turned back and looked him in the eye again. "It's real. It's a relationship with someone who knows what it's like to answer the challenges that life gives you. He lived it. He lived through more suffering and hardship in life than either of us could ever endure. And He did it because He loves us and wants us to know how much He loves us."

"I know a little about Jesus, David. And I know enough that He could never love me after how much I've messed up my life. You? You're different. He could love you. You're . . . perfect."

"That's just it. I'm not perfect. I tried to live like that, but I found out that I can never be good enough to earn God's love. No one can. That's why He sent His son Jesus to die for us, to provide the way for us to live with Him forever. So we wouldn't have to try to be perfect . . . or good enough." She wasn't quite convinced. He lowered his voice and took another step closer to her. "I'm not perfect. You're not perfect. But He still loves both of us." David gently grabbed Joani's hand again. "He loves you, Joani. And I wanted to come here and tell you that . . . as your friend."

She pondered his words. "OK. I'll think about it."

* * * * *

Snake and the lady in red ambled toward the table in the corner. Her high heels made a knocking sound against the hardwood floor as she carried the first of what she hoped would be many complimentary drinks, one in each hand. Snake's boots shuffled against the wood. The two made rhythmic music together.

Snake moved to the chair in between the two women. "Hi. Just in from Indy?" he questioned the woman at the table as he offered to shake her hand. "I'm the welcoming committee." Both girls giggled. "What's your name?" he asked the seated one.

CONVICTION

"I'm Georgia," she whispered.

"And I'm Florida," the red-dress woman said. Snake paused for a moment to see if she was serious. She wasn't. They both laughed and Snake joined in. "That's a little joke we use to break the ice. My name's Kristi, with an 'i.'"

"Well, Georgia and Kristi with an 'i,' how do you like St. Louis so far?"

"So far it looks . . . promising," said Georgia as she winked at Kristi. The girls had come to St. Louis from Indianapolis, where they had escaped a possible prosecution situation. They had thought about Chicago, but decided on St. Louis because neither of them had ever lived there before. No one knew them in St. Louis. And all big cities have sections that offer pretty much the same things: cheap places to live, people who don't ask many questions, and big-ego guys who are willing to fork over cash to sweet, smiling babes.

"So what's your name?" Georgia asked.

"Folks call me Snake."

"Are you a poisonous snake," Kristi responded, "or kind of a pet snake who goes around buying girls drinks?"

"Depends on what you're lookin' for," he said with a smile.

The three laughed and drank for nearly half an hour. Snake drank more than the girls. They knew how to hold their liquor. Snake didn't. He got bold and put his arm around Kristi's shoulder. Georgia made a pouty look and he put his other arm around her and pulled her chair close. She flinched upward as the chair lurched, and then she laughed. Snake had a pretty good idea the girls were playing with his mind and only after his money, but he was having a good time.

They both looked good to him. His money looked *real good* to them.

* * * * *

197

"You'll think about it?" David asked Joani.

"Yeah, I'll think about it," she said.

"Would you mind if I called you sometime?"

"It's a free country."

"Yeah, you told me that on the phone last night."

"I tell that to everyone," she said.

"Shoot, I thought that was something you saved for your close friends." Joani smiled for the first time since David came to the apartment. "There you go. A little smile never hurt anyone."

"Look, you better get out of here. I don't know when Snake is coming back, but you better not be here when he does."

David pulled one of his business cards out of his wallet and wrote down his home phone number on the back. "Here's my card. It's got my work number and my cell number on the front. I wrote my home number on the back. If you ever need anything, you give me a call. OK?"

"OK," she answered, reluctantly, as she put the card in her pocket. "Now get out of here." She pushed him toward the door.

David opened the door and turned to face her. "You'll call me?" he asked.

"Sure. You'll call me?" she joked.

"Sure. That's what friends do, ya know." He smiled and gave a quick wave as he headed out the apartment building to his car.

* * * * *

Carla was wiping down the bar. She fumed about Snake spending money on the two floozies from Indy instead of using that money to pay the rent at Joani's place. How many times had Joani said that she had to work a double shift to make rent because Snake had wasted his money buying drugs? Carla was also confused about the David situation. Snake couldn't have gone to the apartment and found David and Joani together, she hoped. He was looking too smug and cool to have just killed someone. And knowing him, he would have surely done something to David or Joani or both of them if he'd have found them together. She wanted to know for sure, so she came out from behind the bar and approached the threesome at the corner table.

"You all want something else?" she asked.

The three were laughing and having a good time. "Yeah. Sure," Snake slurred. "How 'bout another round? Only this time make it the good stuff. And bring us the bottle." He looked at the girls. "You do shots?" They both giggled.

Carla turned to go back to the bar, but hesitated, turned, and asked Snake, "Hey, isn't Joani supposed to work tonight? I haven't seen her today."

Snake scowled, "Me neither."

"Who's Joani?" asked Georgia, in a fun way.

"She's nothin'," he answered as he turned to Carla. "Where's that bottle?" he growled.

Carla turned toward the bar and the trio resumed their good time. Carla noted the time. It was almost ten-fifteen.

"So, you girls thinkin' about movin' into this neighborhood?"

Georgia asked, "Well, what kind of neighborhood is this?"

"It's *my* neighborhood," Snake boasted.

Carla returned with the bottle of whiskey and three small shot glasses. She placed them on the table and asked Snake, "You haven't seen Joani tonight?"

Disgustedly, Snake responded, "I saw her earlier." He clenched his teeth. "What do *you* care?" He tossed two twenties at her and said, "Keep the change," just to get her off his back.

Carla was still concerned about Joani's situation. Snake had flirted with other women in the bar before, but she knew these girls were going to take it further than the regular clientele. She persisted in the conversation despite the big tip and blurted out, "It's just that some guy was in here earlier lookin' for her."

"A guy?"

"Yeah, some clean-cut guy," Carla said, hesitatingly, as she saw the look of curiosity come over Snake's face. *God, what have I done?*, she thought.

Snake was hoping to score with Georgia and Kristi, but his ego made him curious about the clean-cut guy. He stood up rudely and started walking toward the bar's front door.

"Hey, where you goin'?" Kristi asked. "I thought we was havin' a good time." She was only asking because she was afraid Snake's money was leaving, too.

"I gotta check on something," he sneered. Snake turned toward the front door. Georgia motioned for Kristi to follow him. Their rent money was walking out the door.

"Hey, Snakie, wait up." Kristi stood up quickly and raced toward Snake as he exited the Alibi. She caught up with him on the sidewalk outside and tugged at his coat.

Snake caught a glimpse of a clean-cut guy getting into his car, a late-model tan Caprice. Kristi wheeled in front of Snake and got in his face. "C'mon, Snakie, let's have another drink. The night is still young." Snake grabbed Kristi by the shoulders and pushed her aside to get a good look at the man getting in the Caprice. "Hey!" she responded as Snake shoved her. She nearly tripped on a sidewalk crack. Her high heels clicked on the pavement.

Snake looked at Kristi as the Caprice fired up. She put her hands on her hips and smiled seductively at him. "Is that any way to treat a new girl in town?"

Snake was torn between knowing who the clean-cut guy in the Caprice was and spending more time with Kristi and

Georgia. He glanced back and forth between them. Kristi stood there waiting for an answer. As the Caprice pulled away, Snake noticed the license plate. It read: JTOOLS-1. His mind flashed. He looked at Kristi with a shocked face.

"What's the matter?" she asked.

Snake instantaneously went back to that day at the Gas Stop near Lebanon, and how Joani had left him there, cursing at her, thinking how she and her crazy mind were too much to deal with, and how she had forced him have to figure out how to get back to St. Louis by himself. Then, as if hit by a bolt of lightning, he remembered the license plate. *That guy was there too,* he thought. The license plate! JTOOLS-1. *He must have helped her get away!* The thought of the clean-cut guy returning to see Joani put him over the edge. She was more trouble than she was worth.

Kristi stood there waiting impatiently for Snake to answer her alluring, suggestive stance. Snake turned toward her. "I got some business I gotta take care of." He started walking down the street toward the apartment.

Georgia appeared in the doorway to see how Kristi's charms were working. "We may not be here when you get back," Kristi pouted.

"Your loss," he shouted. But he paused as he spoke . . . and then he came to his senses. He thought so much of his powers over women that he came back to where Kristi was standing. He noticed Georgia in the doorway smiling at him. He was convinced he could talk his way through this and come out a winner. He knew he was powerful enough that he'd be able to bust Joani further into submission and then come back to complete the evening with Georgia and Kristi.

Kristi put her arms around Snake's neck and curled her lips. He put his hands on her firm hips. They felt very enticing. "That's better," she said.

"Look, I gotta take care of something. It'll only take a minute."

Kristi couldn't believe that her charms weren't working on this guy. They had always worked before. Snake could sense that Kristi was losing interest, so he peeled off three twenties and handed them to her. She smiled and closed her hand around them tightly. "I'll be right back," he assured her.

"You bought yourself ten minutes," she said. He peeled off two more twenties and forced them into her fist with the others. Then he pulled her close to his chest and looked into her eyes. If she was afraid of this guy, she didn't show it. She was a pro. "OK, twenty minutes," she said. His bold smile was the last look on his face that she would ever see. He turned and bolted down the sidewalk.Kristi watched Snake march out of sight and then turned toward Georgia, still standing in the open door of the Alibi Bar. She triumphantly held up the cash. "Let's blow this dump, girl."

"You got it," Georgia said. The two walked off down the main drag and into the night.

Snake was more incensed with each step he took toward the apartment. He muttered to himself through his clenched teeth. *What is that guy doing showing up in my neighborhood? Bad enough he messed with Joani back in Lebanon. Probably thinks he's gonna take over here, too.*

He pulled open the front door of the apartment building with ease. Snake was wiry, but stronger than he looked. He took two steps at a time up the stairs to the second floor. He got his keys out of his pocket along the way. He unlocked the door, but Joani had it chained. "Open up," he barked. "Open this door!"

Joani knew the tone of voice. She'd heard it before. He'd been angry with her on occasion about her lipping off to him, or her refusing to cook some dinner on demand. He'd been especially livid after the Lebanon incident, but had cooled down by the time he'd found out her whereabouts and picked her up at the farm. He'd pushed her around some, but for some reason, he'd never hit her. Joani was thankful for that. She knew he'd beaten the tar out of men ten times as strong as she was. He could have really done her some bodily harm, but he was more interested in manipulating her than scarring her.

Joani unchained the door. Snake smacked the door and it swung open and hit the wall with a thud. Joani flinched as Snake yelled, "Who was that guy?"

"What guy?"

"Whaddaya mean 'what guy?' The guy that was up here."

Joani hesitated. There was no getting around the truth. "He's a . . . friend I met a long time ago. That's all."

"He was there the day you left me in Lebanon." He slapped her across the face with an open right hand. Joani gasped with surprise and held onto the left side of her face as she slumped onto the couch in the middle of the room. "What was he doing here?"

She was silent except for her tears. She didn't know what words she could say to change his hostile tone.

Snake slapped her again on the side of her head. Her hair flew up in the air as the force of the blow knocked her over. She bumped the other side of her head on the arm of the couch. It made a thump as it hit the thin, frayed dark green cloth covering that had long since lost its padding due to poor construction and age. She had tears of pain, anger, and frustration already building. Snake growled, "I said, 'What was he doing here!?'"

She sat up quickly and defiantly. "What do you care!" she bellowed. She flinched as he raised his right hand and faked another blow to her already swollen cheek. All of the emotion she felt because of the abuse she had taken at the hand of Snake had finally boiled over. She stood up and pushed the cheap wooden coffee table away from the couch with her foot. "I'm outa here!" she said.

Snake grabbed her by the neck and pushed her back down on the couch. "You're not goin' anywhere."

Joani bounced back up and declared, "Yeah, I am."

This time Snake let her have it. The blow came from the deepest part of his anger. It was a combination of the abuse of his childhood, his lack of any social or employment skills, the squalid neighborhood he lived in, the alcohol he consumed, and the drugs. The drugs had provided the major influence. They had made him an uncontrollable beast, stripped of any conscience. He hit Joani with a clenched fist on the cheekbone directly below her left eye. The quick, powerful blow stunned her. She fell back on the couch. She felt like she was losing consciousness. Just then, the phone rang. *Let it be David,* she thought. *No, don't let it be David!* She was lost and confused and started crying hopelessly.

Snake picked up the receiver. "Yeah?" he said with a snarl.

"Is Joani there?" the female voice asked.

"Not right now. Who's this?"

"This is Carla, Snake. Put Joani on. I wanna talk to her."

"Ya can't right now," he sneered.

"Is she OK? Snake, if you've hurt her . . . "

"Everything's under control. Nothin' to worry about."

"Snake, let me talk to her!"

"Maybe later." He hung up the phone and immediately his mind went back to Georgia and Kristi waiting for him at the Alibi. Joani was now sobbing uncontrollably. Snake didn't want any part of this scene. She was such a pathetic victim, not much of a challenge for his strength. He leaned down and got in Joani's face. "Now, listen good. I gotta go out for a while, a long while. Be here when I get back or you're gonna get worse." He grabbed her chin and lifted her eyes to his. "You hear me?"

"Yeah," she muttered through her sobs.

He straightened up, backed away slowly, and walked out the door, not bothering to lock it.

Joani sat for a moment. The pain in her cheek was monumental. She patted her face to see if he had drawn blood. The only moisture on her face was her tears. She stood up and went over to the door to lock and chain it. *What's the use?* she thought. *He'll just break it down.* Joani caught sight of her image in the dusty mirror on the wall by the door. *What an awful sight*, she thought. She sniffed through her nose, which made the pain shoot through her face. As she stared at her reflection and lightly touched her cheek area, which was swelling her eye shut, she remembered her mother. How many times had Joani seen her mom's face looking like that? Too many times. How many times had her mother warned her not to go down the same path that she had gone down? Again, too many warnings. "Mom, I'm sorry," she whispered out loud. "My life's a mess."

Joani reached into her pocket and pulled out David's business card. She looked at the back, where David had written his home phone number. "I gotta get out of here . . . for good," she said. "David, you're my only hope." She walked toward the table next to the couch, reached for her phone, and dialed David's number.

* * * * *

Snake walked back to the Alibi. With each step out the door he forgot about Joani and thought more about Georgia and Kristi. He stopped and thought maybe he should bring them a little gift. He hustled back to his car and looked in the glove compartment. He pulled out a small bag of white powder. This should be enough for a party of three, he thought. By the time he reached the Alibi front door, he was really looking forward to spending some quality time with the two Indiana visitors.

He walked in the door and glanced around for the two women. They weren't in sight, so he shot straight for the bar.

Carla saw him coming and reached for the wooden baseball bat she kept behind the bar. She was a tough cookie who knew how to use the bat and was more than ready. "Where's those two girls I was with? They in the bathroom?"

"They split, Snake. Soon as you left."

You could do a lot of things to Snake and he might only get mad. But if you messed with his money, you could count on him getting mad and doing something about it. "Where'd they go?"

"How should I know?" Carla barked, the disgust clear in her voice.

Snake leaned toward Carla. "You sure they ain't in the bathroom?"

"Sorry. They split."

"They got some of my money," he barked. He reached out and grabbed Carla by the shirt collar.

Carla wheeled the baseball bat around and slammed it on the bar. "Enough!" she shouted. The whole bar vibrated as she dented the old wooden railing. Several glasses and bottles flipped in the air and clanked as they toppled. One fell on the floor and shattered. The bar customers all stopped and stared at Carla and Snake. "That's enough, Snake! I ain't takin' any more from you!" He released his grip on her shirt. She grabbed the bat with both hands and looked as if she would be more than happy to take a swing at Snake's head; her hands were shaking, but she looked more than ready. Snake backed away from the bar, out of swinging distance, and held his hands up in front of him as if to surrender. "Now, get out! And don't come back. Or I'm gonna call the cops. You hear me?"

"I hear you," he whispered, nodding, as he backed up slowly. "I hear you. I just don't like people stealin' money from me."

"Get outa here," Carla said again.

He turned and left the bar. Carla loosened the tension in her face and relaxed her tight grip on the bat. Three bikers were playing pool. They looked at each other, grinning, raising their eyebrows, and shaking their heads. "Hey, Rocko," one of them said. "Go ask the lady for another round. It's your turn to buy."

"Not me, man. Let's give her a couple minutes."

"God, I hate this job," Carla fumed. "I gotta be nuts to work in a place like this."

* * * * *

Snake had been bested by a woman with a ball bat. There wasn't much worse for a self-centered maniac who thought all women were to be used and abused. To be called down in front of people on his turf was the lowest of lows. *I'll get her,* he thought. *First, I gotta get my money back. Wonder which way those Hoosiers went.*

A timid figure of a man stepped out of the shadows toward Snake. It was A.J., a twenty-four-year-old junkie who lived in the neighborhood and often bought cocaine from Snake. "Snake," he stuttered, "I need some stuff. I got da money. You got anything for me?"

My bad luck just might be turning around, Snake thought. "You sure you got some money, A.J.?"

"Yeah, I got money." He held up some green in his trembling hand.

"Then I got the stuff. How much money you got?"

"I got forty bucks on me right now."

"That won't buy you much, A.J. You're gonna have to come up with at least a hundred."

"OK, Snake. I got the rest back at my place. My aunt got paid today and I know where she keeps her stash." A.J. was living with his hardworking, overly loving, religious-hearted aunt, who thought that if she could only get A.J. turned on to Jesus, that He could clean him up.

Snake sized up the situation. "Your aunt home now?" he asked.

"Nah, she's got a night job on weekends. She won't be back 'til morning."

Snake thought maybe she'd have more than a hundred dollars at her place. He could make a nice profit tonight off this junkie. Snake pulled the small bag of white powder out of his pocket. "OK, A.J., let's go see what your aunt's got stashed. My car's down the street. I'll drive ya."

A.J. grinned at Snake, and Snake grinned back. They each had something the other wanted. It was free enterprise of a dubious sort at work in this part of a very tough neighborhood.

TWENTY-THREE

David pulled into his driveway with a great sense that he had done the right thing in offering his friendship to Joani, but also with the sense that he hadn't done enough. For some reason, he parked the car in the driveway instead of pulling it into the garage. As he shut off the engine, he folded his hands on the top of the steering wheel and prayed. "Lord, did I do the right thing? Did I do enough? Lord, please be with Joani. Help her to know that she does have a friend in me. Help her to know that she can call me." David sighed, knowing for now he had done what needed to be done and that everything else was in the Lord's hands.

* * * * *

Snake parked his car on the street in front of A.J.'s aunt's tiny old modest block home. A.J. hustled out of the car toward the front door. Snake watched him hurry off and then reached into the glove compartment. He grabbed his .38-caliber pistol and checked to make sure it was loaded. *Just in case.*

* * * * *

As David walked into his house and threw his keys on the table near the door, he noticed his landline phone answering machine had one message on it. He pushed the rewind and then the play button. There was a pause, then a sniffle. "David," a voice quivered. "It's Joani. You said I could call you if I needed help. Well, I'm calling. I know you left here a little bit ago, but could you come back and get me?" She paused again. David didn't even hear her final "please" because he had grabbed his keys and was racing to his car.

David weaved in and out of highway traffic at a frantic pace, trying to cover the ten miles back to Joani's downtown apartment as quickly as he could. He knew he was driving recklessly and that there was no plausible excuse for it if he got pulled over by the police—except that he was on his way to help a friend. However, he sensed by the tone on the phone message that Joani was in some kind of deep trouble and genuinely needed his help. Unlike their first encounter at the Gas Stop, when she had chosen him simply because he had the look of a good person, this time she called on him because he was her friend. David didn't know what he could do to help her, or if she would want him to take her somewhere again, but she had enough confidence in him to call, so he knew he had to respond.

Something must have happened, he thought. *I was just there. Something bad must have happened.* David pushed the gas pedal harder and accelerated into the vacant outside lane.

* * * * *

A.J. nervously unlocked the front door of his aunt's home. Snake looked around and cautiously walked in behind him. He didn't want to face the aunt. Not tonight. He'd had enough problems with women tonight. He adjusted the .38 that he'd slipped into his belt to make sure it was ready for a quick defense, but he kept it out of sight behind his jean jacket.

Snake followed A.J. into the kitchen and watched as he reached into a ceramic cookie jar and pulled out a wad of cash. He sorted out four tens and four fives and added them to his two twenties. He put the rest of the money back in the jar and hurriedly handed the cash over to Snake, who exchanged it for the white powder. A.J. disappeared with his purchase into the bathroom.

This is just too easy, Snake thought. He looked toward the cookie jar, knowing he was only a few feet away from the cleanest heist he'd ever been involved in.

A.J. called from the bathroom. "This is good stuff, Snake, huh?"

"Yeah, good stuff." He could hear A.J. inhaling the powder. *This junkie better not OD on me. He's a good customer, even if his aunt is the one who pays for his stuff.* Snake heard nothing more from A.J., so he walked down the hall toward the bathroom. A.J. appeared in the bathroom door. The drugs were already taking effect. He was now smiling and calm. "Ah, yes," he sighed. He sniffed deeply through his nose as he steadied himself on the doorframe.

"You want some, Snake?"

"Nah, I gotta get goin'."

"OK, Snake. Thanks. We'll party some other time." A.J. turned toward his bedroom at the end of the hall and shuffled the six steps to the open door. He flipped on the light, a low-wattage lamp on a nightstand that had a Bible laying on it, and then plopped onto his bed, exhausted but relieved for at least the next few hours. Snake shook his head at the pathetic young man. *Ain't my deal,* he thought.

Snake walked back down the hall toward the kitchen. He passed the bathroom. The bag of white powder was lying open on the sink. *This is just too easy.* Snake grabbed the bag, which still had a couple more rounds of insane relief in it, sealed it up, and stuffed it back in his pocket. Then he set his sights on that cookie jar.

"Must be a couple hundred bucks here," he said softly to himself as he wadded up the money and stuffed it in his jeans pocket. He laughed and shook his head. "Too easy. Just too easy."

* * * * *

David had to be a little more careful once he exited the freeway and drove the streets of the neighborhood surrounding the Alibi Bar. There were cars parked on the street and a couple of children playing in a front yard, even though it was approaching midnight. One of them could easily dart into traffic to chase a ball or something. The kids in this neighborhood were probably used to the hazards of playing near the street, even at this hour. Still, David didn't want anything tragic to happen on his way to Joani's place.

David turned right onto Joani's street at the corner by the Alibi Bar. There was a parking place in front of her building, across the street. He wheeled into it and jumped out, not even bothering to lock his car.

He retraced his steps through the front door of Joani's apartment building that, an hour ago, he had first walked into. Then, he was full of apprehension. Now, he was full of conviction. He breezed by the creaky steps and the drab hallway walls that were yellowed from age. They had frightened him before. Now, they seemed much less intimidating.

* * * * *

Snake drove Joani's Camaro down the dark alley near the run-down apartment he shared with her. With his .38 on the seat next to him, he reveled in satisfaction with the way the evening had turned out. He had two or three hundred dollars of A.J.'s aunt's cash in his pocket along with the excess dope he had sold A.J. He laughed as he thought about the possibility of selling the same junk to A.J. a few days from now.

Even though it was nearing midnight, a young boy was playing basketball on a makeshift hoop nailed to a pole in a driveway. A single light on the brick wall dimly illuminated the court. He shuffled to retrieve a ball that had caromed off a fence and was bouncing toward the alley. The kid stopped short of Snake's car as the ball hit the moving Camaro, startling Snake. His brakes screeched suddenly as the car hit the bouncing ball. The .38 slid off the seat to the floor. Snake slammed his hand down hard on the horn and shouted, "Hey, watch what you're doin', punk!"

The boy never changed expression as he stared at Snake, who passed by, not bothering to stop the car. The boy knew Snake by reputation from the neighborhood, and he knew to stay clear of him.

Snake continued down the alley as the boy retrieved his basketball and went back to his game. As he turned into the street, he spotted a parking place a couple of doors down from the apartment building and across the street. Snake pulled in at an awkward angle, pointing in the opposite direction of traffic. He didn't care. He owned these streets. He fished around in the darkness for his .38 on the floor of the Camaro. Gun in hand, he exited the car. As he crossed toward the apartment building, slipping his pistol back in his belt, he noticed the late-model tan Caprice was back. *He's not stupid enough to come back, is he?*

* * * * *

As David reached for the doorknob with his right hand and began knocking on the door with his left, the door swung slowly inward before he could even call out Joani's name. His hands backed away as the door creaked open. Joani was standing in the middle of the shabby living room. She sniffed through her nose and dropped her line of sight toward the floor. Her long auburn hair was disheveled. Her mascara had run down her swollen and flushed cheeks. David approached her slowly, staring at his marred, injured friend. He gently reached out and lifted her chin upward. Her left eye was nearly swelled shut. She started crying again. "He beat me up. I told him I was leaving him, and he beat me up."

"Where is he now?" David asked while looking around.

* * * * *

Snake paused as he ambled into the middle of the street, but angled back out of an evil curiosity to take a look at the Caprice license plate to make sure it was the same car. The plate read JTOOLS 1. A depraved smile came over his face. "This is gonna be good," he snarled as he bounded toward the apartment building.

* * * * *

"I don't know where he is. He went out on another drug run, I think. I was lucky he didn't kill me first. He got a call that took his attention away from hammerin' on me. Must've been important 'cause he lit outa here quick. But he said he'd be back. I gotta get out of here, David. Please take me somewhere! Anywhere! I got a bag packed. Let's go . . ."

"Oh, ain't this great?" The coarse, low voice from behind

Joani and David startled both of them. They turned abruptly to find Snake standing in the open doorway. He closed the door behind him as he sported an evil, squint-eyed look on his face. He moved slowly toward the two of them; they were frozen in their shoes. "Saw your car out front, *toolman*."

"Snake, just let us go," Joani said, in what was mostly a whimper.

"Shut up." He pointed an angry finger at her and then glared into David's eyes as he paced slowly closer to the two of them. He was like an animal cautiously getting into position to pounce on a prey. David turned quickly to face him head on, keeping himself between Snake and Joani. "So, you're the guy who helped her get away that day on the highway? I remembered that license plate of yours. Now you think you're gonna try and help her again, do ya? They're gonna need some real tools to put you back together again when I get through with you."

Snake reached out to push David with both of his long arms, but David grabbed his dirty jean jacket. They spun around, stumbling, and then released their grips on each other. Snake smiled a sadistic grin as he reached inside his jacket. David caught a glimpse of a small-caliber pistol as Snake pulled it out of his belt. David sprung at him with full force, driving his shoulder into Snake's midsection. The gun dropped to the floor. Joani shrieked as David pushed Snake into the living room wall, knocking down a picture that had been hanging from the dingy wallpaper. He grimaced from the impact, but recovered quickly, grabbing David and spinning him into the wall. "Snake, stop it! Leave him alone!" Joani pleaded.

He paid no attention to her cries. Snake brought his right hand quickly and squarely into David's midsection, knocking the wind out of him. David felt a left fist and then a right one smack the sides of his head. He put his arms up to defend the blows, but over and over Snake flailed his wiry but muscular arms and fists at David. Some of the blows landed on his arms, causing the pain to shoot down to David's fingers and up through his shoulders. The pain seemed to quickly be multiplying. Other punches found their mark on David's head and chest and ribs. This was not a fight. It was David struggling for his very life, and quickly losing the energy to defend himself.

"Snake, I mean it! Leave him alone!"

Snake cursed at Joani through his clenched teeth as he continued his barrage of blows to David's head and arms. "Too late! Nobody . . . muscles . . . in on me . . . and gets away with it." His fists pounded David's upper body indiscriminately with each phrase he slowly spoke. David tried to fight back, occasionally landing a glancing blow of his own. His fists, weak from the pain in his arms and exhausted from absorbing Snake's pounding, barely made an impact on Snake's face and chest. They stumbled around to one side of the living room, bumping into a chair, a table with a lamp on it, and the wall several times. David could feel his face already starting to swell up. He was sure Snake had broken the skin on his face as he could feel drops of blood or sweat—or both— running down his skin.

"Snake, you're hurting him!" Joani's plea fell on deaf, angry ears.

"Thought you could rescue the helpless barmaid?" Snake continued his assault on David's face, the blows coming slower now, but not much weaker, even though he was experiencing his own physical exhaustion. "No way, man! And when I get through with you, she's next!" David was so weak now he couldn't defend himself. He fell to his knees. With both hands, Snake picked David up by his sweat-soaked and bloodied shirt and lifted him to his feet. Snake's left hand steadied David as his right curled back for a final punch. David was helpless to defend this shot. "You're mine, toolman," he whispered as his right fist drove toward the center of David's face. David saw it coming, as if in slow motion, but couldn't stop it. The blow hit him full force on his nose and right eye. He fell backward onto the cheap coffee table in front of the tattered couch. The table smashed into several pieces, the wood fragments digging into his back. His head made a thud as it hit both the table and the floor. David knew he was going to black out and probably never wake up. He tried to force his eyes open. His vision was blurred by sweat. His arms were so weak and exhausted he couldn't lift them to wipe his eyes clean. He closed his eyes tight and tried to open them again. "Oh, God, help me," he prayed.

David caught a view of an equally exhausted but victorious foe reaching for a metal rod in the corner of the room. Snake dragged the rod along the floor, preparing to deliver a deathblow to David's brain. David was too tired to move. He resolved that these were his last moments on earth. The simple man who had lived a boring life up until a couple of months ago was going to meet his end in a violent confrontation with evil personified.

"You're dead," Snake proclaimed through the saliva dripping from his open mouth. His chest was heaving to catch his breath. He slowly raised the rod in the air.

"Oh, God, forgive me," Joani prayed.

The room was spinning. David faintly heard Joani yell Snake's name from behind him. Snake glanced toward her while holding the rod over his head.

Crack! Crack!

Snake staggered backward and hit the wall. He dropped the metal rod and clutched at his chest. Blood was already oozing through his sweat-soaked T-shirt. David strained to turn his head around. He could see Joani holding Snake's pistol, still pointed at him, the smoke curling from the barrel.

David couldn't muster any words. Snake fell to his knees and cursed a last pronouncement of his hatred toward his life, the world, everyone in it, and especially his barmaid roommate. He fell limp, then dead, at David's feet. David breathed what he thought would be his last breath . . . and passed out.

TWENTY-FOUR

David's eyes were still closed. He was aware that he was lying flat—probably in a hospital bed or a morgue if his memory served him right about the beating he'd received. There was muffled movement in the room, but David wasn't curious about who it was. Not yet. He was simply thankful he was still breathing. His head was pounding. He pinched his eyelids to begin the opening process. His facial skin was tight and ached as he squeezed and flinched. He opened his eyes quickly. Water in his eyes made his vision blurred. He blinked several times to clear his sight. *I must be alive*, he thought.

David moved his shoulders. They were still aching, too. He recognized his mom's voice. "His eyes are open, Jack." She came into David's line of sight from over his right shoulder. "He's awake."

David's dad moved into David's sight line from the end of

the bed. "Hey, Son." He reached for the intercom button to call for the nurse. Both of David's parents were leaning over his bed in plain, wonderful sight.

"Hey, Son," Jack repeated.

"Hey," David mumbled.

Tears flowed from his mom's eyes. "We were so worried about you, David."

"What happened?" David coughed with the words and winced from the pain in his face and upper body.

"You got beat up pretty bad, Son," Jack said in a calming voice. "Let's not worry about that right now. Let's concentrate on waking up first."

The nurse came through the door with a concerned look on her face and rushed to David's bedside.

"Mr. Freeman." The nurse spoke in a serious tone. David thought she was talking to his dad. "Mr. Freeman," she said louder; David now realized she was talking to him.

"Uh-huh?"

"How are you feeling?" she asked politely.

"I've got a headache. And I hurt all over. My face hurts."

"You've got several lacerations and contusions on your face." She moved closer to examine David's face. "Do you know where you are?"

"I guess I'm in a hospital."

"Do you know what city?"

"I guess it might be St. Louis. That's the last town I remember."

"Do you remember getting beat up?"

David paused. "Unfortunately, yes."

"Do you remember coming to the hospital?"

"No. I remember Snake getting shot. *Joani!*" David started to raise himself up in the bed. "Where's Joani?"

The nurse put her hands on his shoulders to keep him lying down. "It's OK, Mr. Freeman."

"David, lie still," his mom insisted.

"Yes, Son," his dad added. "Don't worry about anything else right now. You need to concentrate on getting better."

David nestled back into the pillow and the relatively soft mattress. The nurse released her grip and looked to Jack. "I'm going to page Dr. Thompson. It looks like David's come completely out of the coma. Try to keep him quiet. I'll be back in a minute." The nurse gave David another glance and turned to quickly walk out of the room, her new tennis shoes giving a noticeable squeak with each step.

Sylvia patted David on the shoulder. She wasn't able to speak much through her tears except for a muffled "Praise God. Thank you, Jesus."

His dad moved toward the side of the bed and softly said, "Glad you're awake, Son."

"Me, too," David exclaimed. He cleared his throat again.

"You've been out three days, David," his mom said. "We've been so worried about you."

"It's good to see you with your eyes open, Son," Jack said, grinning with approval. "Next time, give me a call. The two of us could have taken him easy." David smiled.

"I've been out three days?" David asked.

Jack carried the conversation. "We got a call from Pastor Mueller about 7 AM on Saturday morning. He got a call from your Pastor Brunette. He didn't know our names, but he knew we went to Chuck's church. So he called Chuck and Chuck got in touch with us."

"We got here as soon as we could. David, how could this happen?" His mom started to cry again.

Jack put his arm around her to reassure her. "Now, Momma, don't get upset. We'll sort out all the details later. Remember, the nurse said not to get him all riled up."

"I'm sorry," Sylvia said as she wiped her nose with a handkerchief. "I just hated the sight of seeing you lying in a hospital bed, David, all cut up and bruised."

"I'm sorry too, Mom. I got caught in the middle of something." He glanced toward each one of them. "What's happened to Joani?"

Jack leaned down. "We met her, here at the hospital. We didn't want to get *all* the details from her. Not yet anyway. She looked pretty scared and worried about you. And we were worried about you. And we didn't want to get into it too much. We figured there'd be time for that."

"Is she the girl you told us about?" Mom asked.

"Yeah. She's the one with the baggage." David squirmed to change position, wincing from the pain all over his body. "She was my friend." He measured each word carefully. "She needed help, and I was her friend, and so I tried to help her. Turns out, she helped me."

"You did a good thing, David," his dad assured him. "She was in yesterday, but she had to talk with the police again this morning."

"The police," Sylvia murmured, then turned away.

"The police wanted to talk with her about what she knew about that roommate of hers and his connections."

"Is she in trouble?" The thought struck David like a brick. "My God, she shot Snake!" His mind started racing. "She killed him. He is dead, isn't he?"

Jack moved in to subdue the conversation. "Calm down, Son." He paused. "Yes, the guy is dead. She might be in some trouble, but I think they've already figured it was self-defense. They got your face as evidence." He smiled, and so did David.

Sylvia slapped Jack on the shoulder. "I just don't understand you two," she sobbed.

"I'm sorry, Momma," Jack said. "Maybe this isn't the right time for it."

"Of course it isn't the right time. We almost lost our son," she scolded.

"It's OK, Mom." David turned his head toward her. "A little humor is probably what I need right now."

"David, this has been really hard on me. I didn't raise you to run around with *criminals*." She whispered the word: *criminals*.

Jack put his arm around Sylvia again to calm her down. "Yes, but you did raise him to help someone in need. He did a good thing. It just didn't turn out good for him right now. But thankfully, he's awake, and hopefully he'll get better really quickly and make a full recovery." He looked closely into Sylvia's eyes. "OK?"

"OK," she sighed.

"We better let David get some rest now," his dad said as he turned to David. "We'll go get some lunch and come back a little later, David. You rest."

"OK," David said. Jack and Sylvia looked around the room as if to see what they would need to gather up before going to lunch. David blurted out: "Thanks." They turned to look at him. "Thanks for being here."

His mom moved close. She smiled through her tears and kissed David on top of his head.

"We'll be back in a little while. You rest," Dad said.

As they started for the door, each one glancing back to smile and wave, David inquired, "Hey, what day is it?"

"It's Tuesday," his dad offered. "Cubs are in New York tonight."

"Does this place have cable?"

"What do you think we've been doing the last three days while you've been sleeping?"

Sylvia slapped Jack on his shoulder again to punish him for his comment. Jack shook his head and gently pushed Sylvia out of the room, turning to David. "We'll be back later . . . if they let us come back."

David smiled, breathed a sigh of contentment and relief,

and burrowed into his bed. The pain was still real, but so was the prospect of healing. He knew he was surrounded by his parents who loved him and his God who had given him an opportunity to live another day.

* * * * *

David met Dr. Thompson. He pronounced him "recovering nicely" and "lucky." David told him he agreed with the recovering part, but he didn't feel very lucky. He considered it more like being blessed that God had given him some more time to live. The doctor nodded and murmured "Uh-huh," while he wrote notes on his clipboard.

David dozed off several times during the next few hours. He was awakened by a gentle hand touching his arm. His eyes opened and there was auburn-haired Joani Givens breaking into a quiet smile. "Hi," she whispered.

"Hi." David was really glad to see her. She couldn't hide the telltale marks on the left side of her face from the beating she'd received from Snake, but David looked past her bruises and caught a small glimpse of her heart through her eyes and her sympathetic smile. He tried to sit up, but was still unable to put much weight on his elbows to raise his own battered body.

"Just lie still," she insisted. She reached for a short stool with wheels on it and rolled it next to the bed. She sat with her head level with his and rested her arms on the cool metal sides of the hospital bed. She winced slightly as she laid the left side of her face on her arms so they could look each other in the eyes. "I'm sorry, David." He tried to assure her that she didn't need to apologize, but she wouldn't listen. "I got you into this mess. I nearly got you killed. It's all my fault."

"I volunteered right from the start. I could have driven on by the rest stop that first day, but I didn't."

Joani raised her head up and chuckled. "No, you didn't. You

jumped on the roller coaster and zoom—there we went." She smiled as she swept her hand from right to left. Her smile, however, was quickly replaced by a sober frown. "David, I didn't think you'd ever have to tangle with Snake." She paused, running the sordid events quickly through her memory. She lowered the metal side rail on the bed that blocked their complete view of each other's faces. "I don't know what made me think I could ever get away from him."

"It took a lot of courage to do what you did," David said.

"To shoot him?"

"You gave him every chance in the book to stop beating the tar out of me. And look what he did to you!" Joani stood up and turned to walk a couple of steps away from the bed. "Joani, it was self-defense," he said.

She turned back and whispered, "I never wanted to kill him." Her eyes filled with tears. "David, I killed him." She rushed back to the bed and laid her head on David's arm, sobbing. He stroked the back of her head and realized it was the first time he had touched her beautiful auburn hair. She rose up quickly, knowing she had to be aggravating his bruises. "Oh, I'm sorry. Did I hurt you? I'm always hurting people."

David grabbed her hand before she could move away from him. "It's all right. *You* didn't hurt me." She put her other hand on top of his.

"You're a nice guy, Dave. Why are you so nice to me?"

He measured his words as they stared into each other's eyes. "It's a free country," he blurted out.

Joani released a beautiful and unexpected laugh through her tears. It was the resonance of hidden joy rising from a secret part of her heart. They had only known each other for a couple of months, and this was the first time he had ever heard a sound like that emanating from her spirit. Her eyes sparkled and her smile brightened her whole face. "David, I haven't laughed like that in a long time," she said. "We just don't laugh like that in my neighborhood."

"You could move, you know."

"Actually, I am getting out." She piqued his interest. "I'm going to spend some time at the farm again. Only this time, June and Herb said I should check out getting into an alcohol program in Springfield. They found this outpatient thing, and they say it's a good one."

"That's a good thing," David said.

"And June and Herb also said I could stay with them as long I make the effort to go to church with them. I think maybe it's time for me to check out this Jesus you talked about the other night."

"That's an even better thing," David said. "What about the police? Are you in any trouble?"

"The police said it was self-defense, me killing Snake. He wasn't as big of a dealer as he thought he was, but he knew some people. I gave them what names I knew. The cops checked up on me with the other girls who worked at the bar. They vouched for me that Snake handled his business by himself, and that I wasn't involved. They let me off, but they did say I should probably leave town for my own safety. I've been staying with Carla from the bar the last couple of nights. I wanted to make sure you were OK before headin' to the farm. So, you doin' all right?"

David hesitated answering, thinking she might turn and take flight out the door right then and there if he said he was doing fine. "I'm going to be OK. I think I need a little time to recuperate," he said.

After a moment of silence, they realized they were still holding hands and looking into each other's eyes. They each released their touch as they sensed that they were violating some code of friendship ethic, diving into areas they were either not allowed to, or not ready to plunge into.

Joani changed the subject. "I met your parents." David acknowledged the switch with a nod. "They were really nice to me, too."

"They're good people. I've known 'em all my life." That peaceful and joy-filled look came over her face again because of David's attempt at humor.

"Get out of here." She slapped David on the arm and then realized what she did. "Oh, I'm sorry. Did that hurt?" They both laughed, and Joani sat down on the stool again and held onto his arm. They both ventured back into the uncharted waters of closeness. It was awkward, but pleasant. Joani whispered, "Maybe you could come visit me sometime . . . at the farm . . . near Springfield."

"I'd like that," David said. She concurred with a nod of her head. "Sure. I'd like that," he repeated.

"Me too," she replied.

"We could talk," he added.

She countered with, "or take a walk . . . or something."

They sat in silence for several seconds that seemed like minutes, or even longer. Joani stroked David's shoulder and he touched the back of her arm. They smiled at each other. She would look away and then glance back again. He stared at her face and then broke the silence. "Could you come a little closer so I could kiss you?"

"Don't your lips hurt?"

"I won't know until you kiss me," David said.

Joani slowly rose up off the stool and maneuvered her face over his. Her auburn hair fell off her shoulder and brushed the side of his face. She closed her eyes, gently placed her lips on his, and gave him the "first kiss" he had dreamed of. She backed away for a second as both of their eyes opened and met, so close, so quietly passionate. She kissed him again a little longer, a little harder. It was very nice . . . for both of them.

She sat on the stool again.

David remarked, "Now I *definitely* know I'm coming to

"You sure?" She cocked her head coyly to one side. He nodded that he was sure. Joani sighed, "The adventure begins again, eh?"

"It never stops," he said. "Besides, who would ever want to live a life that's boring?"

AUTHOR'S NOTES

Several events in this book are taken from my actual life experiences, including my childhood, as I spent many joy-filled days on my grandma and grandpa's farm just south of Mattoon, Illinois.

Lebanon, Missouri is an actual town along I-44; I'm not sure if it has a drug problem among its teenagers and young adults or not. However, if there is one person doing drugs in any town, it is a problem and should be a concern of its citizens.

It just so happens that Lebanon was the city where I saw the auburn-haired girl. Yes, I did actually see an auburn-haired girl in a black Camaro at a gas station in Lebanon, Missouri. She didn't ask me to meet her at a rest stop, but that's where the whole story got started in my mind.

As far as I know, there is no Alibi Bar in St. Louis. I love St. Louis, Indianapolis, and Chicago. Like all big cities, they each have their good and bad areas. I will admit, though, that I find driving in Chicago a difficult experience. My hat's off to all of you who must drive those roads every day. You are exceptional human beings.

Thanks to Pastor Chuck Mueller and his parishioners at Trinity Lutheran Church in Roselle, Illinois; and to Pastor John Brunette and the members of his church at Faith Lutheran Church in Oakville, Missouri (a suburb of St. Louis) for the use of their names. They both are fine pastors and both are fine churches. I have worshipped in both places and would recommend them to anyone.

Thanks also to Paul and Angela Brunette. They really do invite people over to their home for Sunday dinner, and I was fortunate enough to be one of those people one Sunday. The story about their daughter Christina's illness is true, and you can read more about their Basket of Hope ministry at www.basketofhope.org.

Thanks to Joe White of Kanakuk Kamps ministries and James Ryle of Truth Works Ministries for their inspiring presentations at the Promise Keepers rally in Jackson, Mississippi.

And thanks to Promise Keepers men's ministry (www.promisekeepers.org) for inspiring me to relate the experience of the character David Freeman through the context of one of their rallies. It is an adventure that has been duplicated in many men's lives in many different ways through the years. I have attended several Promise Keepers rallies and I plan to go again and take other men with me. I highly endorse their ministry.

And thanks to Coach Bill McCartney for listening to God when He gave you the idea for PK and for following through on the concept of holding major arena events where men could join together to be encouraged to make commitments to God, their wives, their families, and each other. I remember when Coach Mac came up with the idea in the mid-seventies and expressed it to all of us at the coaches' prayer breakfast in Ann Arbor, Michigan. Thanks for dreaming, preparing, and then taking it to the field, Coach.

ACKNOWLEDGEMENTS

Thanks to Jenny Cote for introducing me to her agent, Paul Shepherd.

Thanks to Paul Shepherd for reading my novels The Lost Principled Man and No White Lies and catching my vision for this book series called The Legacy Circle. And for taking my ideas to Larry Carpenter.

Thanks to Larry Carpenter for his publishing and marketing expertise and his willingness to take on another writer and attempt to put him into a position to succeed beyond his current circle.

Thanks to Bob Irvin for a wonderful editing job. Your tweaks took this book from 211-degrees to 212.

Thanks to Suzanne Lawing and Lori Martinsek for the artwork and design modifications to make this book look so professional.

Thanks to everyone for reading this book. I hope you are encouraged to follow Jesus through your own adventures.

Thanks to my wife Leslie for believing in me and encouraging me to keep writing.

Thanks to Jesus for all the rescues in my life and for pulling everything together.

So from now on we regard no one from a worldly point of view. Though we once regarded Christ in this way, we do so no longer. Therefore, if anyone is in Christ, the new creation has come: The old has gone, the new is here! All this is from God, who reconciled us to himself through Christ and gave us the ministry of reconciliation: that God was reconciling the world to himself in Christ, not counting people's sins against them. And he has committed to us the message of reconciliation. We are therefore Christ's ambassadors, as though God were making his appeal through us. We implore you on Christ's behalf: Be reconciled to God. God made him who had no sin to be sin for us, so that in him we might become the righteousness of God.

II Corinthians 5:16-21

Since Jesus went through everything you're going through and more, learn to think like Him . . . Then you'll be able to live out your days free to pursue what God wants instead of being tyrannized by what you want.

I Timothy 4:1, 2 (The Message)

Conviction (The Journey of a Lost Principled Man) is the first of five novels by Don Wharton in a series titled "The Legacy Circle" that centers on the character of David Freeman. In this first book, David is twenty-five years old and experiences a coming-to-faith moment. In the second volume, *No White Lies*, David, now forty, has the opportunity to strengthen his faith through several challenging situations. The third novel, *The Hossmen*, deals with fifty-five-year-old David as he reunites with the high school friends he played baseball with, and as he faces his most daunting life test.

The fourth and fifth novels planned for this series are still being developed. Lord willing, we will see them happen.

* * * * *

Don Wharton has made appearances in all 50 states and three foreign countries as a singer, songwriter, humorist, and filmmaker.

For more information on Don's ministry, including how to order copies of this book and other items, check out his website at:

www.donwharton.com

You may also write to Don at:
Don Wharton
P.O. Box 15201
Fort Wayne, IN 46885